MILAN GOTCHER

The Outward Shows the Least

RAMBLING
BEAR
PUBLISHING

First published by Rambling Bear Publishing 2025

This novel is entirely a work of fiction. The names, characters, and incidents portrayed in it are the work of the author's imagination. Any resemblance to actual persons, living or dead, events, or localities is entirely coincidental.

Milan Gotcher asserts the moral right to be identified as the author of this work.

First edition

ISBN: 979-8-9939817-0-3

This book was professionally typeset on Reedsy.
Find out more at reedsy.com

Contents

Prologue

The stone walls seemed to breathe in the dark. Brother Russo felt it as he worked late in the archive room, a barely perceptible shift in the old masonry that made the shadows pulse. Winter wind hammered the cliff outside. Inside, the air didn't move.

His camera flash lit the foundation stones in sharp bursts. After six months documenting the monastery's architecture, he had finally found them, symbols cut into the oldest stones, nothing like any Christian imagery he recognized.

"There's a pattern," he muttered, copying photos to his laptop. The screen lit his face in blue. Sleep had been getting harder since he started spending his days down here.

The generator hummed somewhere in the building, feeding the sparse wiring. When the lights flickered and held, Russo zoomed in on a particularly detailed mark. His fingers felt strange on the keys when he worked with these images. He'd been trying not to notice that.

Then the stonework on his screen went wrong. The carved design appeared to shift between frames, the lines slow and liquid across the surface. He blinked hard and blamed the hour.

"Just need sleep," he said to nobody.

A low-battery warning. The laptop had been plugged in for hours. Russo checked the cord, which was secure, and the battery kept draining anyway, as though something were drawing power directly from the unit.

He bent toward the outlet, and a photograph on the floor caught his eye. It had fallen from the desk. The image on it was not the foundation he'd shot that morning. The pattern was different. More deliberate. When he tried to trace the geometry with his finger, the lines seemed to avoid his focus.

"That's not possible," he said, and meant it.

The monitor began breaking apart. Distortions spreading through his files, not random static but something that moved with intention. In each photo of the foundation stones, new marks had appeared. He had not taken those photos. Nobody had.

Russo had graduate degrees in theology and archaeological preservation. He'd been sent here because the church trusted him to be careful. Science and faith had always held together in him, not easily, but they'd held. As the lights flickered again and stayed off a fraction too long, he felt something inside him shift.

"Brother Russo." Abbot Kyrillos, from the doorway. The old man was barely visible, his face lit only by the glow of Russo's dead screen.

Russo startled badly. "Father. I was only…"

"The foundation stones." Not a question. The Abbot's pale eyes caught the dark the way cats' eyes do. "I told you to focus on the manuscripts."

"I found repeated symbols, Father, symbols that predate the monastery. They appear to form some kind of…"

"I know what they form." The Abbot moved into the room with a smoothness that didn't belong to a man his age. "You are not the first to find them interesting."

Russo tried to respond and found the words had left him.

"Six monks, in my lifetime." The Abbot's voice went quieter

and somehow larger. "Six. All of them gone, one way or another, once they'd finished their work. So you will focus on the manuscripts, unless you're hoping to be the seventh." A pause. "You look like you haven't slept. Go to bed. This will still be here tomorrow."

Russo nodded. He packed up without arguing and followed the Abbot out.

He went back three nights later.

His audio recorder caught the scrape of his footsteps on the stone stairs hidden behind the old cellar, steep and narrow, cut into rock. The flashlight threw wobbling shadows over walls that glistened with slow seepage.

"Third night of unusual readings," he said into the recorder. "EMF spikes near the north foundation wall. Temperature drop of roughly fifteen degrees near the anomaly, consistent regardless of outside conditions."

He kept to the clinical language. It helped. The sense of control it gave him was probably false, but he needed it as he descended further than any of the current brothers had gone. His research over the past three days had turned up only fragments. Sealed chambers, a crypt referenced in the oldest records as containing "that which cannot be destroyed." Nothing more specific than that.

He moved down a narrow corridor, cold stone on both sides, the air thick with a smell like centuries of extinguished candles. His fingers trailed along carved figures worn smooth by time. Then he felt a draft, thin but steady, in air that should have been still.

It led him toward the chapel's far wall. Not a decision, exactly, more like something obvious. His palm against the stone found a seam. He moved a heavy tapestry aside. Behind it was a door

3

he hadn't known was there, and behind the door was a set of stairs going down into nothing.

He went in.

The temperature fell with each step. His breath fogged. The flashlight batteries dropped fast, faster than made sense, and when he switched to his phone, it began dying just as quickly, its screen strobing between normal display and something that looked like the symbols upstairs.

His foot found bottom. The passage opened into a small antechamber. His light fell on walls dense with carved marks, the same symbols he'd been photographing but larger here, cut deep into stone that seemed to pull at the light rather than reflect it.

"The symbols are stronger here," he said to the recorder. His voice came out lower than he'd meant it to.

Between the symbols, a door. Its edges were packed so tightly with carved lines that they appeared as a single continuous mark.

He walked toward it. The symbols moved at the periphery of his vision, slow and fluid, stopping the moment he looked directly at them. His equipment was giving impossible readings. Then his phone screen went dark.

Complete darkness.

He heard his own breathing, too loud. And under it, from behind the door, something else. Slow and even. Rhythmic. Something breathing back.

He snapped three chemical lights at once. Green light filled the antechamber. The symbols on the walls seemed to hover.

The sound grew.

"Hello?" he called, and immediately felt the mistake. His voice returned distorted, the room's acoustics wrong in some

4

way he couldn't explain.

Nothing answered. But the certainty of being watched became something he could no longer argue himself out of.

He raised his camera. The viewfinder was static. He took the photo anyway.

The flash showed him a crack. Running straight down the center of the door, fresh and clean through old stone. From it, something dark was seeping through, not air, not liquid, moving like both.

The chemical lights died at once, together, like a switch thrown.

"The seal is breaking from inside," Russo said into the recorder, his voice too high and too fast. "Something's wrong with the door."

He stepped backward, and his heel caught the bottom stair. In the cracks, the dark seemed to concentrate.

He turned and went up. Three steps, four, five. The stairs kept extending ahead of him, multiplying, refusing to end.

"Stay back," he said, though there was nothing to say it to.

Behind him, a rushing sound. The floor of the chamber.

You know why you're here. The questions you can't answer. The emptiness that drove you to these walls.

He felt the voice as pressure behind his eyes. Not sound. Just understanding, placed there.

He kept climbing, scattering gear behind him in the dark.

We see the shadow you carry. We've been waiting for someone shaped like you.

The cold was inside his chest. The dark was pressing against him, not metaphorically, with actual weight against his skin and face.

"I serve God," he said, and heard how small it sounded.

You came before us. Light came after us. Come with us now.

The darkness moved up his body. He hit the wall with both hands, stone where the passage should have continued. Trapped.

"What do you want from me?" he whispered.

To fill what is broken in you. To make it something that lasts.

He saw things then. The people he had walked away from to enter the monastery. The faith crisis that had sent him to archaeology, searching for evidence in old stones because belief had stopped being enough. Wherever he was hollow, the dark knew. It was offering to pour itself in.

His breathing changed. The terror was still there, but something was rising through it that he didn't want to name.

"This isn't real," he said. His voice was barely there.

Your wounds prepared you. We only come for the ones who are ready.

As the darkness reached his face and found his mouth, Russo tried to pray. The words dissolved. Something cold and vast filled the space where his lungs had been.

His last words were on the recorder, and barely legible, "It was waiting. All this time. For someone like me."

Then a sound like exhaling.

Then the recorder ran for another six minutes, capturing nothing but the silence of the room.

Chapter 1

Marcus Stavros's hands shook as he worked through the photographs scattered across his desk. The scanner hummed to his left, its green light crawling over another photo of the monastery foundations. Three years ago, those same hands had waved victoriously in front of packed lecture halls. Now they trembled with exhaustion and something closer to anger.

The wall clock read 7:54 AM. Six minutes before his classroom door opened.

He heaved himself up and smoothed his rumpled shirt. The hallway outside was already loud with student chatter, but it would go quiet the moment they saw him. Dr. Marcus Stavros, once the department darling, was now its cautionary tale.

At 8:00 exactly, he opened the door. Six students. A new record, even for him.

"Good morning." His voice echoed off the vacant walls. "Today we'll be discussing the excavation of the Pythian Apollo temple."

A phone came up. Someone coughed. Two students in the back row were already zipping their backpacks. Marcus clicked to the next slide, but the projector stuttered, and for one awful moment, the image that appeared was not the temple. It was a slide from three years ago. The foundation stones of St. Nikolas Monastery.

Three years dissolved. The heat of the stage lights at the Athens Symposium, the expectant murmur of a thousand colleagues. He had been at the peak of his career, presenting the core of his life's work. Then the moderator called for questions.

Victoria Nash had risen from the front row, her voice cutting through the applause. "A fascinating, if speculative, interpretation, Doctor," she began, her tone balanced between professional respect and dismissal. "But where is the empirical rigor? You present these architectural anomalies as a language, yet you offer no key, no Rosetta Stone. You're asking us to leap from architectural curiosity to a conclusion of cosmic significance, without the proper methodology, or any documented methodology at all."

The room shifted. Doubt, once planted, spreads fast. He fumbled for a response, but she had already won. The pitying looks from colleagues, the quiet closing of notebooks, the way everything he had built collapsed in about thirty seconds.

His fingers found the remote. The monastery image disappeared. When he looked up, the two backpack students were gone.

"The structural integrity of the temple foundation," he started, then stopped. The girl in the front row wasn't even pretending. Her phone screen lit up her face, some video playing, her expression blank.

"That's all for today." The words sat wrong in his mouth. "Chapter four for next week."

The room emptied in seconds. Marcus stood at the chalkboard, sweeping away chalk scraps with slow, even strokes. His hand passed over the brass plaque on the podium, "Donated in honor of Dr. Marcus Stavros, Distinguished Chair of Archaeological Studies, 2018."

"Your students seem especially alert today."

Victoria Nash stood in the doorway. Silver hair pulled back in a French twist, fitted blazer, posture perfectly straight. That slight smile that never reached her eyes.

Marcus didn't look over. "Is there something you need, Victoria?"

"Just checking on the digitization project. The department needs those documents by the end of the week."

"It's on track."

"Good." She stepped into the room, heels clicking on the linoleum. "We wouldn't want your enthusiasm getting in the way of proper procedure. Again."

He gathered his things without answering. Victoria had taken him apart carefully, never accusing him directly, only planting doubt in the right places at the right times. Now she sat behind the desk that used to be his.

"There is one thing, actually," she said as he moved toward the door. "The new research program I'm running. Pre-Christian religious sites in Greece. Familiar territory, I'd imagine."

Marcus's grip tightened on his briefcase. "You're following my research locations?"

"Following is a bit strong. I prefer properly documenting."

He turned to face her. "You know I was right. That's why you're…"

"What I know," Victoria said evenly, "is that extraordinary claims require extraordinary evidence. Something you never quite managed to provide." She paused at the door. "Get those scans done, Marcus. Some of us have actual work to do."

After she left, Marcus went back to his office, a converted

storage closet that smelled of cleaning fluid and stale air. The monastery photos sat in a pile on his desk, each one a fragment of the argument he'd been trying to finish for three years.

He fed another photo into the scanner and watched the green light move across it. Then he saw it. A shape in the foundation that had no business being there. He fed in more photos, his pulse quickening. Three different monasteries, hundreds of miles apart, all showing the same impossible structure.

His phone buzzed. Helena's face on the screen, his ex-wife, the third time this week. He let it go.

He spread the photographs across the desk, his hands steadier now. The designs were subtle, easy to miss unless you knew what to look for. Unless you'd spent years being dismissed at conferences for suggesting that Christian monasteries had been built on older sacred ground. Unless you'd staked your career on the idea that the ancient Greeks had left something encoded in stone.

He picked up his phone and scrolled to a number he hadn't called in years. Father Antonios had been one of the few who'd taken his work seriously without mockery. Maybe he still would.

The digitization project could wait. Victoria could wait. The bank account and the ruined reputation could wait.

In the faded photograph of St. Nikolas's foundation stones, Marcus could make out symbols that predated Christ by a thousand years. Symbols that suggested the monastery hadn't been built to glorify God, but to contain something that came before it.

He thought about Victoria's new research program, the way she'd built her career on the wreckage of his. Let her chase her documented hypotheses. He might have already found what actually mattered, written in stone that the field had mostly chosen to ignore.

Marcus picked up a red pen and wrote one word on his office window: VINDICATION?

He stared at it, then erased it. Not yet.

Tomorrow, there would be another empty classroom. More of Victoria watching him from doorways. Tonight, though, he had the photographs spread out in front of him, patterns on ancient stone that nobody else was looking for.

His hands were completely still. He hadn't felt this way in three years.

Chapter 2

The Kymolos morning ferry battled rough seas, its deck slippery with spray. Marcus clutched the rail as the monastery came through the fog. The limestone structure seemed to erupt straight from the cliffside, as if it had grown there rather than been built.

An elderly woman clutched her worry beads, praying softly as the monastery came into view. The other passengers gave it a wide berth, crossing themselves when they thought no one was looking. Only Marcus stared directly at it, taking in the peculiar shape of the structure.

By the time they docked, storm clouds had gathered over the shoreline. The first large drops of rain began to fall as Marcus shouldered his pack and started up the rise.

The path was treacherous. Switchbacks carved into the rock had turned to mud, and his boots slid with every step. His rental car, parked at the harbor, would never have made it up here. Only stone steps worn smooth by centuries of pilgrims, and a feeling he couldn't quite shake that he was being watched.

Lightning split the sky as he reached the monastery doors. A young monk appeared through a side door before Marcus could knock.

"The monastery is closed, sir." The monk's accent was heavy

but clear enough. "Evening prayers have begun."

"I've come to see Abbot Kyrillos." Marcus pulled a plastic-covered photo from his jacket. He glanced at it briefly before holding it out, the two of them at an Athens conference, back when his ideas still got him into rooms. "He'll remember me."

The monk took the photo and went inside without a word. Marcus waited in the rain, water running from his hair, until the door opened again.

"This way."

Candlelight. Dancing shadows on the walls. The monk led him through corridors that bent in unexpected directions, past openings that went dark almost immediately.

They stopped at a plain wooden door. The monk knocked twice and stepped back.

"Enter."

Abbot Kyrillos sat behind a simple desk, exactly as Marcus remembered. White beard, blue eyes that didn't give much away. One candle on the desk.

"Dr. Stavros." The Abbot's voice was quiet but carried. "You've arrived at an interesting time."

"The rain came out of nowhere." Marcus set his dripping pack down. "Thank you for seeing me."

"The weather." The Abbot kept his eyes on Marcus's face. "Yes. It has been. unusual." He nodded toward a chair. "Show me why you've really come."

Marcus spread the photos across the desk. "See these patterns? They appear in monasteries all over Greece. Including yours. I was hoping you'd let me examine the ones here, and..."

"Let me tell you a story first." The Abbot picked up one of the photographs and held it to the candlelight. "There was a village not far from here. The villagers drew water from a well for

13

generations, until one day the water came up dark. Not muddy. Almost black. As if they were drawing up shadow itself."

Marcus leaned forward.

"They sealed it with mortar and stone. Now their children carry water from the valley." The Abbot set the photo down. "Some wells go too deep, Dr. Stavros."

"But these patterns…"

"I know what they are." The Abbot drew out an old leather journal. The pages cracked as he opened it, and Marcus caught a glimpse of diagrams nearly identical to his photos before the Abbot closed it again. "As did my predecessor. And his before him."

"Then you know I'm right. The monasteries were built on pre-Christian sites. They're connected to something."

"They're a matter of protection." The Abbot's tone changed. "Not all knowledge belongs in academic journals."

Thunder moved through the building. In the flash of lightning that followed, Marcus saw something shift in the shadows behind the Abbot. A shadow that seemed too solid to just be the absence of light.

"I need to reach the foundations," Marcus said. "Just long enough to document…"

"Pride comes before the fall, Dr. Stavros. And you've already fallen a great distance, haven't you?"

That one caught him off guard. "This has nothing to do with my work."

"Hasn't it?" The Abbot moved to the window. Outside, the sea was dark and loud. "You came here with equipment, with theories, wanting confirmation. But what will you do once you find what you're looking for?"

"Record it. Publish it. Prove that…"

14

"Prove that you were right all along?" The Abbot turned back to him. "Let me tell you about Brother Russo."

Marcus frowned. "Who?"

"He was here six months ago. Also interested in the foundation stones. Also certain he could untangle old mysteries." The Abbot's eyes caught the candlelight. "We gave him room to work. And one day we found his gear in the lower chambers. Nothing else. We never found him, or the others before him who came looking at old drawings on the walls."

A chill moved through Marcus that had nothing to do with his wet clothes.

"Some doors," the Abbot said, "once opened, don't close again." He pulled a sheet of paper from the desk. "I will give you one day. Tomorrow. You may document the outer foundations. You will not go below. You will break no seals. When the sun sets, you leave."

"That's not enough time, Abbot. A week, please."

"It is all the time you will have." The Abbot began to write, his hand moving in neat Greek. "Brother Andreas will take you to the guest quarters. In the morning, he supervises your work."

Marcus knew when a conversation was over. He gathered his photos, noticing how the Abbot's gaze stayed on one image longer than the others. A pattern of stones spiraling inward.

"A week, fine. No more, though," the Abbot said, almost to himself.

"Thank you. We'll be in and out, you'll see."

"One more thing," the Abbot said as Marcus reached the door. "The patterns you've found. They aren't messages from the past. They're warnings. The question isn't what they were trying to say. It's what they were trying to contain."

Brother Andreas waited in the hallway holding a lamp that

15

threw long shadows across the walls. As they walked, Marcus noticed things he'd missed on the way inside. Scratches in the stone that looked almost like claw marks, doors with locks on the outside, and a faint smell of something burning everywhere.

The guest room was bare but clean. When Andreas lit the candle, Marcus saw something on the small shelf, pushed behind a Bible. A diary. Water-damaged cover.

"Kitchen accounts," Andreas said, and picked it up before Marcus could reach it. "Very boring."

Marcus had already seen the first page. A diagram, identical to his foundation patterns. The handwriting was a script he didn't recognize. Two words in English at the bottom.

It watches.

After Andreas left, Marcus lay on the narrow bed and listened to the storm. Somewhere in the monastery, bells began to toll. Not the call to prayer. Something else, older. And the sound seemed to rise from below rather than above, as if the bells were buried somewhere beneath the floor.

Brother Russo's gear, left in the lower chambers. Wells that pulled up darkness. Warnings, not messages.

He had a week. He'd need to pull his team together fast, but it could work. It had to work. Beneath these stones, something was waiting to be found.

The candle went out. The room went dark. In the quiet, beneath the bells, he heard something else. Slow. Patient. Like breathing from very far below.

He reached for his flashlight. Dead batteries.

Marcus pulled the thin blanket up and lay there, listening, trying very hard not to think about Brother Russo.

Chapter 3

Niko arrived twenty minutes late, sliding into the booth with practiced ease. Three phones materialized on the table like playing cards.

"Finally ready to admit you need your little brother's help?" He flagged the bartender without looking up from his screens. "Macallan 25 for me, Jack for him. Still drinking that swill from college, right?"

Marcus's jaw tightened. Some dances never change. "Actually, I've switched to..."

"Saw your leave of absence announcement." Niko's thumb never stopped scrolling. "Brutal timing with the housing market. But I might have something, grunt work on a preservation project. Can't have my brother starving out there."

The assumption that he'd been fired shouldn't have stung, but it did. Marcus let it pass, falling into their old rhythm. "Still turning ruins into resorts?"

"Someone has to pay the family bills." Niko straightened Marcus's collar with automatic precision, the gesture both affectionate and condescending. "Show me what you've got."

Marcus opened his laptop and angled it toward Niko. His brother's eyes tracked the screen with surprising focus.

"Prime location," Niko murmured. "Religious zoning's tricky

though, but with the right incentives, hmm."

"Look at the markings on the foundation." Marcus zoomed in. "The erosion patterns are wrong. See these cracks? Too deep, too regular. Like something pushed through from the inside."

For a moment, Niko's hand stilled on his glass. Between them hung their grandmother's stories about Greek holy places, old warnings about churches built to keep things in rather than let them out.

An email notification lit up Marcus's screen: "Helena Stavros — Re: Monastery Research."

"Still uses her married name?" Niko's eyebrows rose. "In her professional email? Interesting."

Marcus locked his phone, but it buzzed immediately with a video call. Helena's face filled the screen, reading glasses perched on her nose, hair escaping from its clip the way it always did when she was deep in research.

"Marcus!" Her voice was urgent under her usual professional tone. "I found documents about that monastery. You need to see this."

"Still on that?" Niko leaned back.

Helena's eyes sharpened. "Must be nice, having better things to do than help your brother."

"Must be nice, inserting yourself into our family business post-divorce."

"Both of you." Marcus's voice was flat. "Focus."

"I'm coming there," Helena said, already gathering her things. The call ended.

Niko chuckled, reaching for the check he'd pre-written. "She hasn't changed a bit."

"Neither have you." Marcus gathered his materials. "Still

trying to buy your way into conversations."

"Still convinced you're one discovery away from vindication." Niko produced a contract from his leather portfolio. "Lucky for you, I already drafted terms. Full funding for your expedition."

"In exchange for what?"

"First rights to develop any non-historical sections of the site." Niko's grin turned wolfish. "Someone has to think practically."

Helena arrived like a storm, messenger bag bulging with documents. She pulled a chair over and spread papers across the table without ceremony.

"The monastery's foundation goes deeper than any records show." She laid out ground-penetrating radar images. "These scans show chambers below the known structure. Massive spaces that…" She frowned at the data. "That seems to shift position between scans."

"Measurement error," Niko said. "Happens all the time."

"Look at the timestamps." Helena's finger traced the anomalies. "Same equipment, same operator, minutes apart."

Marcus felt his pulse quicken.

"The last several research teams reported equipment failures," Helena continued, spreading incident reports across the table. "Electronic malfunctions, compass anomalies. And personnel disappearances."

"How many?" Marcus kept his voice level.

"Seven confirmed missing. Three others were found in states of severe psychological distress."

Niko's phones buzzed in sequence. He glanced at them, then back at the radar images. "You're telling me there's a basement that plays hide and seek?"

"I'm telling you something down there doesn't want to be found." Helena met Marcus's eyes. "But you're going anyway."

It wasn't a question.

"He has to." The mockery had left Niko's voice. "It's who he is. Who he's always been." He looked at Marcus. "Remember that summer in Crete? The cave system grandmother warned us about?"

The memory came back sharp and physical. The smell of damp earth. The weight of the stone above him. The chamber they'd found was wrong in some way he still couldn't name... walls carved with patterns that seemed to shift just past the edge of the flashlight beam. At the center, the darkness was absolute, light just swallowed, and Marcus had felt an almost physical need to step in, to understand what was there. Niko had been terrified. He'd grabbed Marcus's arm and pulled them both back to the surface without a word, his grip hard enough to leave a bruise. He never went underground again. Marcus had spent years trying to find a way back.

"This is different," Marcus said.

"It never is." Niko pulled out his checkbook. "You see patterns where others see rocks. You follow them regardless of consequences." He signed with a flourish. "At least this time you'll be properly equipped."

Helena leaned forward. "I'm coming with you."

Both brothers said it at the same time, "No!" They looked at each other.

"I have the technical expertise. I've studied the architectural anomalies. And someone needs to keep you from doing something spectacularly stupid."

"It's dangerous, Helena," Marcus started.

"So was our marriage. I survived that."

Niko laughed despite himself. "She has a point."

Marcus looked between them. His brother, who built his

empire on other people's ruins. His ex-wife, who'd always understood his obsessions better than he wanted her to. Neither of them should be here. Both of them were going to come anyway.

"Fine." He turned to Helena. "We follow my lead underground."

"Agreed." She was already marking up Niko's contract, red pen moving fast. "No development rights until we understand what's down there."

Niko sighed. "No trust in family."

"You tried to buy your brother's research," Helena said. "Twice."

While they argued, Marcus studied the radar images. The chambers shifted in patterns he was starting to recognize... not random drift, not measurement error. Something else. Something that had its own rhythm.

His phone buzzed. Unknown number, but the Greek was formal, deliberate, "Some doors, once opened, change those who pass through. Consider carefully who you bring to the threshold. —K"

Abbot Kyrillos. Whether that was a warning or an invitation, Marcus couldn't tell. Maybe there wasn't a difference.

"Marcus?" Helena touched his arm. "You all right?"

"When do we leave?" he asked.

"I can have everything arranged by Tuesday," Niko said. "Boat, equipment, permits..."

"Monday." Marcus closed his laptop. "We leave Monday."

"That's three days," Helena said.

"Then we'd better get started."

Chapter 4

Elena Papadakis's office was a corner room on the seventeenth floor of Quantum Engineering's Athens headquarters, the only room with its blinds always closed. Through the frosted glass, Marcus could see her moving in tight, repetitive loops, checking something, adjusting something, checking again.

She didn't look up when he entered. Three monitors, each showing the earthquake simulation from a different angle. Her fingers moved across a custom keyboard, adjusting variables that never adjusted the outcome.

"A few more minutes," she said, one finger raised. "The simulation has to finish its cycle."

Marcus looked around while he waited. Framed degrees and news clippings covered the walls, side by side, "Engineer's Early Warning Saves Dozens" next to "Athens Earthquake: What Went Wrong?" A laser measure sat within easy reach, its case covered in safety stickers. No furniture touched load-bearing walls. Clear paths to both exits, emergency supplies in the corners.

When the simulation ended, Elena finally turned. Dark circles. The scar above her left eyebrow stood out white against her olive skin.

"Dr. Stavros. Your message mentioned underground chambers."

Marcus spread the photographs across her desk. "These support configurations shouldn't exist. The space below reads larger inside than outside."

Elena's fingers traced the edge of a photo. Her breathing changed. "These load distributions are impossible. The monastery should have come down centuries ago." She pulled up her analysis software. "Unless…"

"Unless what?"

"Nothing. A mistake." Her hand went to her scar before she seemed to realize it, the one she got pulling a child from the rubble seconds before the second collapse.

"I need someone who can make sense of these structures," Marcus said. "The images don't add up. I think there's something underneath all of it, and I need your help to find it."

She turned back to her screens. "I don't do field work."

"Please, Elena."

"What's there?" She spun around. "According to these scans, what's there can't exist. Chambers that violate basic geometry. No support columns. Stone that behaves…" Her voice caught. "Solid one moment, flexible the next."

Thunder outside, though the sky had been clear all day. Elena's instruments registered a tremor so faint that nothing else would have caught it.

"Did you feel that?" Her knuckles went white against the desk.

"Feel what?"

"Never mind." She let her hands go. "This is exactly my point. I see failure in every stress point. I can't turn it off."

Marcus leaned forward. "What if that's what I actually need?"

23

Elena looked at the photos again. Her fingers were already moving toward her keyboard. "Helena's radar shows them shifting position?"

"Between scans. Like the stone is fluid."

"Stone doesn't do that." She overlaid the patterns anyway. Athens bedrock, twelve hours before the quake. Microfractures were moving and reorienting along stress lines. The resemblance was right there.

"If I go," she said slowly, "I control all safety protocols. No arguments."

"Agreed."

"I mean it. When I say we leave, we leave."

"Understood."

She was already thinking through equipment and exit routes. She hadn't said yes yet, not in so many words.

"One more thing. The teams before us, the ones that disappeared. Their last recordings showed equipment failures consistent with localized electromagnetic anomalies. Same signature as what we picked up before the Athens building fell."

"You think it's connected?"

"I think some things repeat." She pulled out a tablet. "If we do this, we will be prepared for everything."

After he left, Elena sat alone, watching the building fall on a loop. Three years hadn't changed the ending. Maybe this time was different. She pulled up Marcus's photos and started cross-referencing, the patterns already surfacing, patient as anything, waiting for someone to look.

Thunder again outside. This time she didn't flinch.

Father Thomas Rivera was kneeling in the basement chapel of the Vatican's Archaeological Institute when Marcus arrived, rosary beads moving through his fingers. Afternoon light through the stained glass fell in colors across his head.

Marcus waited in the doorway. He didn't know why, but the stillness in the room was a relief.

"Dr. Stavros." Father Thomas rose smoothly and pocketed the rosary. "Punctual as promised."

They sat in a nearby pew. Marcus laid the photographs out and watched Thomas's face as he went through them. At the first symbol, something in the priest's neck went tight.

"These markings." His finger hovered without touching. "Pre-Christian. But worked into the Christian architecture, as if the builders were constructing around something already there."

"That's my theory. The monasteries went up on top of existing sites."

"Sacred to whom, though?" Thomas pulled out a notebook dense with sketches. "I've encountered similar symbols in early burial sites. Always somewhere, people reported things they couldn't explain."

His left hand shook as he sketched. He caught it and held it still.

"What kind of things?"

"Voices in empty rooms. Shadows going the wrong direction. Always the feeling of something watching. Something older than the Church's presence there." He looked up. "Why do you need a priest? This sounds like a job for archaeologists."

"Because the Abbot at St. Nikolas warned me about doors that

25

shouldn't be opened. I need someone who takes that seriously and can also tell me what it means."

"Wise man, your Abbot." Thomas's hand moved to his temple. "Some doors close behind you."

"You sound like you know."

The smile was tired. "Thirteen years ago. A house that should have been empty."

He didn't continue. Marcus didn't ask. He could read it in how the fingers found the rosary again without Thomas looking down.

"I need someone who can move between the academic and the spiritual," Marcus said. "Someone who knows that some things don't fit neatly into either."

"Truth." Thomas laughed, soft and worn. "I spent years after divine truth. Turns out some of it comes through darker doors." He looked at the photographs again. "These binding patterns. They're not ornamental. They're meant to hold something."

"Hold what?"

"That's what we'd be going to find out." He stood and moved toward the altar. "Give me three days. There are texts in the restricted archives I want to check. If these symbols are what I think they are, academic credentials won't be enough. We'll need faith."

"In what?"

"In something. Anything. Down there, something to believe in might matter more than you'd expect."

As Marcus collected the photos, Thomas said, "One question about your team. Has anyone been through something serious? A loss, guilt, something they barely survived?"

Marcus looked at him. "Why?"

"Because these sites..." Thomas touched one of the photographs lightly. "They supposedly draw that kind of person. Call to whoever's carrying something heavy. And if I'm right about what these symbols are holding back, that's worth knowing before we go."

He didn't finish the thought. He didn't need to.

That evening, Marcus sat in his Athens office with the personnel files spread around him. Elena and her three minutes. Thomas and his empty house. Helena, still carrying the marriage Marcus had gradually wrecked. Niko, his brother, is still trying to put things back together that Marcus had knocked over on his way out.

And Marcus himself, the failed academic whose obsession had been thorough in its destruction.

He picked up his phone. The Abbot's message was still on the screen, "The foundations remember all who have looked too deep."

Chapter 5

The air in the University of Athens natatorium burned Sarah Chen's nostrils. Chlorine. Always chlorine. Voices ricocheted off tile walls, instructors barking corrections she no longer heard.

She gripped the cold bench at the pool's edge, knuckles white against the blue tile. Her shoulders hunched forward, spine curved away from the water behind her. Three years, and she still couldn't look at it. The surface would be shimmering. Beckoning. She knew without looking.

Instead, she tracked the divers through their reflections in the high windows. Bodies twisted against a grey sky, entering frames of glass and vanishing. Clean. Precise. The way she used to move before her body forgot how.

Her wetsuit hung behind her office door, a stiff black effigy she hadn't touched since the recovery team brought it back. The streak of white cutting through her black hair caught the fluorescent lights above.

A young diver stood poised on the highest platform, alone against the concrete ceiling. The ambient noise seemed to drop away. He leaped... a clean swallow dive. He hit the water with a sound that tore through her defenses. A sharp, percussive thump-hiss as the body pierced the surface, then the muffled roar of collapsing bubbles.

The splash cracked through the natatorium. Sarah's vision tunneled. The tile beneath her blurred into black water, seven hundred meters of it pressing down on her chest. Her ears filled with a sound that wasn't a splash at all but rock groaning, the cave exhaling before it swallowed everything whole.

David's light. She could see it. A steady yellow beam cutting through ink, forty meters below her fins. His hand swept left, pointing into a passage their charts had missed. The beam swung back to her. Not frantic. Excited. He kicked forward.

The cave groaned again.

His light faded. Shrinking from flashlight to candle to star. A pinprick swallowed by black so complete it had texture, weight, hunger.

Gone.

Sarah's body jerked. Her hand clamped around her wrist, nails digging into the watchband until pain cut through the memory. Cold metal under her thumb. The bezel clicked as she spun it. Once. Twice. 2:47 PM. Eleven forty-seven UTC.

Three years. Her lungs still couldn't quite remember how to fill with air.

"Dr. Chen. Thank you for seeing me."

The voice cut through. Marcus Stavros sat beside her, though she hadn't heard him approach. He had the look of a man who had chased a theory so far it had started chasing him back. She knew that look. David had worn it in his final days.

She didn't turn. "The answer is no."

"I haven't asked anything yet."

"You don't have to." Her voice was flat. "Underground chambers. Unexplored water features. A team of academics who need someone with cave diving experience." Her watch

29

caught the light as she finally faced him. "The answer is still no."

Marcus didn't flinch. "It's not just about the diving. Some of the spaces in our scans can't possibly exist without there being more we're not seeing. And you have the skill to navigate unknown waters."

Sarah's laugh came out hollow. "Spaces that shouldn't exist." Her fingers found her watch again.

"The underground tunnels in the monastery flood regularly," Marcus said. "But the water behaves unusually."

"Unusually, how?" She couldn't stop herself. The scientist in her wouldn't let it go.

"Ground-penetrating radar shows it flowing upward in some places. Existing in chambers surrounded by solid rock. Appearing and disappearing between scans."

Her professional instincts fought the cold dread in her stomach. "Water doesn't behave that way."

"No," Marcus agreed. "Something isn't adding up."

He spread photographs on the bench between them. Despite herself, Sarah leaned in, her trained eye catching details others would miss. Stone, but the story was water.

"The mineral deposits suggest flow from multiple directions at once. And these formations…" She stopped. A chill moved through her. "They look organic. Like something grew them rather than natural accretion."

"Helena's scans show chambers that flood and drain without any apparent source."

"Unlikely." But even as she said it, Sarah remembered. The way the cave in Crete had seemed to breathe around them, pressure changing with no discernible cause. David's frantic signals as his compass spun, needle chasing a north it couldn't find.

"I can't," she said, pushing the photos away. "Find someone else."

"There is no one else with your specific expertise. Underwater archaeology, geological analysis, and experience with environments that don't follow the rules."

Sarah's hand tightened on her watch. "You know what happened in Crete."

"I know you survived seventy-two hours in conditions that should have killed you in three."

"I survived because I left David behind." The words came out flat, the way she'd said them a thousand times. "Because when the cave started closing, I swam for the surface instead of going back for him."

"The recovery team said the passage had collapsed. There was nothing…"

"The passage was clear when I looked back." Her voice dropped. "I saw his light below me. Saw him pointing deeper into the cave, like he'd found something. And I left him there."

"If you join us," Marcus said, "you control all underwater operations. Everything."

"There won't be any underwater operations because I won't be there."

But her eyes stayed on the photographs, tracing the water patterns.

"One consultation," he offered. "Review our equipment lists, suggest safety protocols. If you still say no, I won't contact you again."

Sarah checked her watch. Then checked it again.

"One consultation," she said. "But I'm not going underground. And I am never going underwater again."

Three hours later, Sarah stood in Marcus's makeshift office surrounded by equipment manifests and geological surveys. Her resolve had lasted less than five minutes. She'd already reorganized their entire diving gear manifest and added seventeen items they'd missed.

"Your rebreathers are the wrong choice for enclosed spaces with unknown gas compositions," she said. "And these digital depth gauges will be useless if the EM interference is as strong as Elena's data suggests."

Helena nodded, taking notes. "What would you recommend?"

"Analog backups for everything. Mechanical pressure gauges, magnetic compasses sealed in copper housing, and…" Sarah caught herself. "But you won't need any of this, because there won't be any diving."

"Of course not," Helena said smoothly. "But if you were to encounter flooded passages?"

"You retreat. Immediately." Sarah's tone didn't leave room for debate. "Water in a cave isn't just an obstacle. It finds ways through rock that shouldn't exist. It creates passages and closes them. And sometimes…" She stopped. They all felt the unfinished sentence. "Sometimes it keeps what it takes."

Elena arrived that afternoon. The two women didn't say much at first, but they found each other quickly… the quiet recognition of people who had survived something and knew better than to explain it.

Elena tapped her tablet. Numbers scrolled across the screen, jagged peaks and valleys in green. "Look at the electromagnetic readings. Right before the collapse."

She swiped to a second graph. Same jagged pattern, different date. "Crete. Your dive. The frequencies match."

Sarah studied the comparisons, the fear pushed back behind the science. "The patterns are identical. As if both locations were responding to the same stimulus." She shook her head, touching the white streak in her hair without thinking. "This is exactly why I can't go. I'll see patterns that aren't there. I'll jump at shadows."

"Or you'll recognize a real danger the rest of us would miss." Father Thomas had come in quietly, and no one had noticed. "The things that have hurt us... sometimes they teach us to see."

"Is that what we're calling survivor's guilt now?" Sarah said. But she didn't move.

The afternoon bled into dusk. She was elbow-deep in Elena's equipment bag, fingers working through O-rings and pressure gauges without thinking. Her hands knew the sequence. Check the seal. Test the valve. Read the PSI. She heard herself explaining backup protocols, redundancies within redundancies, while some part of her brain reminded her she'd sworn never to touch this gear again.

"The monastery's lower chambers," Marcus said, breaking in. "If they're flooded..."

"When they're flooded," Sarah corrected automatically. "These formations only occur with periodic water exposure. The question is whether it's groundwater, sea infiltration, or..." She hesitated. "Something else."

"Something else?"

"Seven hundred meters down in Crete, we found freshwater pools miles from any source. The water was old. Older than the limestone holding it. And it flowed up. Against gravity. Through passages that opened and closed." Her throat tightened. "Like breathing."

She grabbed her notes. The cave pressed against her memory. "This is why I can't help. I'll twist your data. I'll see intention where there's only chemistry. I'll tell you the cave is alive when it's just rock doing what rock does."

She was halfway to the door when Helena spoke. "What if you're not twisting anything? What if Crete is exactly why we need you?"

Sarah stopped. Her hand hovered over the door handle. "You don't know what it was like. Three days in those cramped spaces. Breathing shallow to conserve air." She turned. "And the worst part? I want to go back. I need to know what my husband saw. What could make someone swim deeper when safety was above him?"

Thunder cracked overhead, loud enough to rattle the windows. The lights flickered, and for a moment, Sarah could have sworn she smelled saltwater.

"One week," she heard herself say. "Surface support only. If there's any diving required, you find someone else."

Marcus nodded quickly, before she could take it back. "Surface support only."

She knew it wasn't true even as she agreed to it. Something was waiting under that monastery… something that would know her. The part of her that had crawled out of Crete alive, that had felt impossible things in the dark. It would have questions. She was afraid she might finally want to answer them.

The others filed out. Chairs scraped. Voices faded down the hall. Sarah stayed. The geological charts spread across the

34

table, blue lines tracking underground rivers flowing the wrong direction. Her finger followed one path, then another. The patterns moved like the water in Crete. Spiraling. Breathing.

Her watch clicked. The bezel turned past the hour. Eleven forty-seven UTC came and went.

She didn't look down.

Chapter 6

Victoria Nash watched Marcus cross the quad three stories below. In the window's reflection, her silver hair caught the afternoon light. Perfect. Controlled. Every strand in place, just like the committee votes she'd lined up against him, the funding she'd redirected, the reputation she'd dismantled one careful cut at a time.

The door hinges whined. Her assistant's footsteps stopped just inside the threshold. "Stavros pulled together a solid team. Elena Papadakis from Quantum Engineering. Some Vatican priest. And that marine archaeologist. The one from the Crete thing."

Victoria didn't turn from the window. "Yes, I'm aware."

She moved to her desk, fingers drumming against the polished surface. Three years ago, she'd taken Marcus apart piece by piece. Every conference presentation questioned, every paper challenged, every funding source pulled away from him. All through legitimate academic critique, of course. The fact that it had cleared her path to department head was merely... fortunate.

"Shall I contact the ethics committee about Dr. Stavros's unauthorized use of university resources?"

"No." Victoria pulled up the monastery photographs on her

screen, the same ones Marcus thought he'd kept to himself. "Let him think he's operating freely. For now."

The patterns were real. She'd seen them during her own quiet visits to the archives, traced them with her own fingers on photographs Marcus didn't know existed. But Marcus would see proof of his theories. She saw leverage. Let him crawl into whatever hole waited under that monastery. Let him risk his neck, his reputation, his sanity. He always pushed too far. Always. And when he did, when he finally broke, she'd be there with proper documentation, proper methodology, proper credit.

The discovery would eventually have her name on it.

"Schedule a meeting with the Hellenic Archaeological Service," she said. "Express my concerns about the expedition's safety protocols. Suggest that oversight might be... prudent."

Her assistant smiled. "Of course, Dr. Nash."

Alone again, Victoria looked more closely at the patterns. In her research, she'd come across the same symbols scattered across the Mediterranean. The written records showed a gap wherever expeditions had failed, knowledge pushed underground.

She unlocked a drawer and removed a file she'd never shown anyone. Her mentor's notes from thirty years ago. Dr. Elisabeth Cray, who'd followed the same patterns until her sudden retirement. The final entry still made her uneasy, "Some doors must remain closed. I was wrong to think academic glory was worth any price. Let this be my warning."

But Elisabeth hadn't had Victoria's advantages. She hadn't learned how to let others take the risks while she claimed the rewards.

Her phone buzzed. The university board had confirmed her

new research grant. Funding that should have been Marcus's was redirected to her "proper" investigation of pre-Christian sites. She'd follow in his footsteps, but carefully. Academically. Letting him clear the path through whatever waited ahead.

Victoria smiled at her reflection. Marcus thought this was about proving his theories. He had no idea he was simply her stalking horse, drawing out into the open what she would eventually claim.

It had never really been about destroying him. It had been about using him.

And he was playing his part perfectly.

Maria Kostopoulou had turned her hospital room into a war room. Photographs covered the walls, the bedside table, and the windowsill. Artifacts arranged in rows, grouped by era and site, and the patterns carved into their surfaces. She pressed one hand against her bandaged ribs as she shifted to watch Marcus come in.

"Morphine makes me useless," she said instead of hello. "So, I'm not taking it. My eyes still work."

She pointed to a photo taped above her IV stand. The monastery foundation, limestone eaten away in radiating circles. "This erosion is wrong. It spreads outward. Like something pushed through from underneath." Her fingernail tapped the center. "I've seen it before."

"Where?"

Maria pulled her hospital gown up to her sternum. Bandages wrapped her torso in white layers, gauze stained yellow at the edges. "The thing that did this. We cataloged it as a Mycenaean carving. Inert stone. I was cleaning oxidation from the surface when it moved."

"Moved how?"

"The stone flowed. Like wax under heat, except cold to the touch. It formed shapes. Reached for me." She touched the bandages over her lowest rib. "Stone that stopped being solid."

Marcus stepped closer. Her notes covered the bed tray. Chemical formulas, temperature graphs, and symbols sketched in a shaking ballpoint that matched the photographs from his monastery.

"These binding patterns aren't art. They're engineering. Containment." Maria's finger traced a repeating glyph. "Sometimes the containers fail."

"You think the monastery is a container of some kind?"

"Yes, and a large one." She swiped her tablet. Side-by-side images filled the display, different sites, same patterns. "Every location with these markings has incidents. Disappearances. Equipment failures with no explanation. Witnesses who say the stone moved."

"I need someone who understands this. Who's survived it?"

She laughed, then sucked air through her teeth as something pulled inside. "You need someone whose organs are still in the right places."

"I need someone who lived through the impossible."

Maria studied him with eyes that had stopped blinking. "You're collecting us, aren't you? The engineer who saw it coming. The priest carrying a ghost from his past. The diver who swam back alone. And now me. The woman who learned that some things don't want to be studied."

"You've been researching my team."

"I research everything. It's why I'm alive." She gestured at the photographs spread across every surface. "The artifact attacked in a pattern. Mathematical. Predictable once I saw the sequence. Your monastery will be the same. Dangerous, but knowable."

She held up her discharge papers. Already signed. "I need a few days to set up the portable medical equipment. Find painkillers that don't fog my head." Her gaze held his. "And Marcus? If these stones move, we're not going to stop to watch. We're going to run."

"Agreed."

"No. You're lying. You think you'll convince me later. That curiosity will win when the moment comes." She pressed her palm against the bandages. "It won't. I already paid to learn that lesson."

The team was fully assembled for the first time in Marcus's temporary office, a space too small for six people, each carrying their own shadow. Elena had placed herself between two exits without seeming to notice she'd done it. Sarah kept checking her dive watch. Father Thomas worked his rosary. Maria cataloged every surface. Niko lounged with practiced ease, but his eyes tracked each person the way he probably tracked investments.

"We leave in three days," Marcus began, but stopped as everyone turned toward the door at once.

Helena stood there, arms full of documents, looking exactly the way she had during their marriage. Hair escaping its clip.

Glasses sliding down her nose. Her mind was already three steps ahead of the conversation.

"Don't mind me," she said, taking over a corner desk. "Just the legal framework keeping you all out of liability lawsuits."

"Helena…"

"The permits are a mess, Marcus. The monastery requires special dispensation, the Greek authorities want archaeological oversight, and someone," she looked at Niko, "already started negotiating development rights for a site we haven't even surveyed."

"Forward thinking," Niko protested. "Market opportunities don't wait."

"For what? For your brother to die in a collapsing ruin?" Helena's tone could have etched glass. "Sit down. All of you. If we're doing this, we're doing it properly."

She'd researched each team member, identified their specialties, and put together documentation that somehow satisfied both legal requirements and their unusual circumstances.

"Dr. Chen," she said, sliding papers across. "Liability waivers that acknowledge pre-existing trauma without voiding insurance coverage. Dr. Papadakis, make sure the equipment transport permits include your specialized sensors. Father Rivera, Vatican diplomatic provisions. Don't ask how I managed that."

"And me?" Niko asked.

"You get to sign promises not to sell anything until we understand what we're dealing with." Helena's smile was sharp.

The planning session stretched into the evening. Elena spread schematics across the table while Sarah marked backup protocols in red pen. Their heads bent together, voices low, debating oxygen reserves and decompression schedules. Across the room, Father Thomas traced his fingers over photographs of Byzantine inscriptions while Maria explained conservation techniques, one hand pressed to her ribs between sentences. Even Niko proved useful, translating their scientific needs into budgets and timelines with the efficiency of someone who moved money for a living.

But Marcus watched the spaces between them. The way Sarah's hand drifted to her wrist when Elena mentioned deep water. How Father Thomas's fingers found his prayer rope whenever Maria described the artifact's attack. The careful distance Niko kept from any photograph showing underground spaces.

They weren't connecting over skills. They were recognizing each other's damage. Everyone in this room had been broken by something that shouldn't exist. And those breaks lined up too neatly with the patterns carved into monastery stone, as if the expedition hadn't chosen them at all.

As if something else had.

Thunder rolled across Athens as evening came on. Sarah's weather equipment, which she had of course brought to an indoor meeting, showed clear skies.

"Atmospheric anomaly," she said, but her hands tightened on the instruments.

Elena's structural sensors confirmed it. "Pressure waves without a source. Electromagnetic fluctuations matching..." She trailed off, comparing data. "Matching patterns from all our incidents. Athens. Crete. The Vatican archives."

"It knows we're coming," Father Thomas said quietly.

No one asked what "it" was.

Maria spread the photographs out again, arranging them until the patterns became legible. Not random architectural details, but parts of something larger. A mechanism built into stone and faith, designed to hold something that had been pressing against its walls.

"Whatever's down there," she said, "it's been waiting. These patterns show stress building over centuries. The container is failing."

"Or being opened from within," Sarah added, remembering caves that breathed.

"Then we stop it," Marcus said, and even he heard the uncertainty in his own voice.

"No." Helena's correction was quiet but firm. "First, we understand it. Then we decide what needs to be done."

When the meeting ended, each person left with their assignment and something harder to name. Not just a job to do, but a feeling of being fitted to a purpose none of them had chosen. As if their separate wounds were pieces of the same pattern, and the pattern had always been pulling them here.

The call came just before midnight.

Victoria Nash watched Athens glitter below, the city laid out in blocks of yellow light and shadow. Her reflection hovered in the glass. Silver hair twisted tight against her skull. Silk blouse pressed flat, every seam sharp.

The phone rang three times. She answered. "Yes."

Her informant moved through names and details. Someone close enough to Marcus to know his plans, resentful enough to pass them on. She didn't need a face. Just the information.

She moved to her desk without sound. The stylus scratched

across her tablet as each name became a note, a weakness, a point of pressure.

Elena Papadakis. The Engineer. She wrote *Survivor's Guilt*. Over-cautious under pressure.

Father Thomas Rivera. The Priest. Sealed military file. Hands shake when stressed. She wrote: Guilt. Can be worked through faith.

Sarah Chen. The Diver. Crete survivor. Avoidance patterns. She wrote *Flight Risk*. Necessary but unstable.

Alexis. A new name. Unexpected. The Guide. She wrote *Familial loss*. Searching. Emotional center. Weak link.

"And the Stavros family," she said into the phone. "Helena handles the legalities. Niko provides the money. How theatrical."

She hung up without a goodbye. The information settled into the sterile air.

Marcus was predictable. Gathering his damaged people, convinced their scars made them wise. He'd always been like that, mistaking survival for insight. Victoria knew what pain produced. Patterns, exploitable ones. Weakness dressed up as experience.

Her eyes moved to the second monitor. The monastery photographs glowed on the dark screen. The same images Marcus thought were his alone. She'd had copies for weeks. The patterns carved into those foundation stones spoke a language she'd been learning in private for years, long before Marcus had stumbled onto them with his theories and his hope.

She opened a private directory. Research files filled the screen, cross-referenced with care. Buried inside was a scanned document. Her mentor's final notes. Dr. Elisabeth Cray's handwriting, normally precise, sprawled in frantic loops across the page. The final entry still made Victoria's spine tighten.

Elisabeth had retired a week later. Gone quiet and never spoken again. She'd seen something and looked away. Victoria had taken the lesson her mentor couldn't. Never be the first one through the door.

She dialed from memory. The line answered on the first ring.

"Director Koulis."

"Victoria." His voice warmed immediately. The Director of the Hellenic Archaeological Service owed her favors he'd never fully repay. "Working late again."

"A concern has come up regarding the Kymolos monastery expedition."

"Ah. The Stavros business. Irregular, but his brother's money opened doors."

"Exactly my concern." Victoria let two seconds pass, then spoke again. "I've reviewed the team. The lead engineer has documented anxiety issues. The diver was the sole survivor of a fatal incident. The whole group is compromised. Sending them into an unstable site without oversight isn't just irresponsible, it's a liability."

She could hear Koulis absorbing it, the doubt settling where she'd planted it.

"What are you suggesting?"

"Official observation. For their safety. A formal request from your office to the ethics committee, citing concerns about procedural integrity."

"Cautious." He tested the word. "Yes. I'll have the paperwork ready by morning."

"Thank you, Director."

She hung up. Satisfaction settled over her. The first net cast. By the time Marcus and his idealists reached the monastery, bureaucracy would already be grinding against them. Operating on borrowed time, under scrutiny. The pressure would make them reckless.

Victoria turned back to the window. The city lay below in its ordered grids of light.

Marcus thought this was about discovery. He was wrong. It was a strategy, and he was part of it.

Chapter 7

The journey to Kymolos was not a voyage. It was a summons.

They moved under a bruised twilight sky, the sea churning metallic grey below. The chartered boat cut through the waves with grim, relentless purpose. No idle chatter. No reviewing of notes. They were past that now.

Elena stood at the stern, gaze fixed not on the churning wake but on the horizon ahead. The scar above her eyebrow was gone, but she still felt it, some ghost of the woman she'd been days ago. The constant anxiety, the obsessive need to check every structural variable, had been replaced by a strange, cold clarity. She could feel the island before she could see it. Something in the way the waves broke against its unseen shores was wrong.

Beside her, Alexis scanned the horizon with the practiced eye of a guide, though he wasn't looking for landmarks. He was reading the patterns in flocking seabirds. The unnatural stillness of the air. The way clouds seemed to part around the island, giving it a wide, fearful berth. His brother's compass, now repaired and resting against his chest, was no longer a navigation tool. It pointed steadfastly toward the island, needle trembling.

The island broke the horizon. A jagged black tooth against dying light. Ancient limestone cliffs erupted straight from the sea, clawing at the sky. Perched atop the highest peak, a wound in the stone, was the monastery. It didn't look built. It looked grown. A cancerous, geometric formation that defied everything organic around it.

The ferry carrying their heavy equipment met them in the choppy harbor. As they transferred crates, the local crew worked with sullen, fearful efficiency, eyes carefully averted from the clifftop. An elderly woman clutched her worry beads and prayed softly under her breath. When she saw Alexis looking, she grabbed his arm.

"The mountain dreams." She whispered in rapid, frantic Greek, eyes wide with a fear older than memory. "It dreams of those who are broken in the right places. It calls them home. Do not listen."

She scurried away, crossing herself as though she'd touched something profane.

The ferry slammed through waves that hit like fists. Salt spray lashed the deck where equipment crates sat strapped and shaking. Marcus gripped the rail as Kymolos rose out of the mist, limestone bleached white against the storm clouds that had chased them from Athens.

Below, a police cruiser's blue lights strobed across the empty dock planks.

Elena stood beside the equipment, one hand on her laser measure, the other braced against a support pole. Each wave lifted the deck, and her shoulders went rigid, though her face stayed blank behind the professional mask of someone assessing cargo straps.

"The straps will hold," Father Thomas said beside her. "I

checked them myself."

"The load distribution is uneven. One sharp wave and…"

"Then we'll deal with it." Sarah moved to Elena's other side, steady despite the rough seas.

Local passengers crossed themselves as the monastery came into view through the spray. The ferry crew kept their eyes on the water.

Police Chief Dimitris waited on the dock, mustache trimmed sharp despite the early hour. His handgun sat wrong on his hip, too large for an island this small. "Papers. All permits and authorizations."

Elena had the folder out before Marcus could move, documents organized with the efficiency of someone who'd anticipated exactly this. The chief opened it, expecting academic chaos. Instead, he got flawless paperwork.

Alexis appeared from the cargo hold, speaking rapid Greek with the dockworkers. Conversations died when he mentioned their destination. An elderly woman grabbed his arm, whispering urgently before scurrying away.

"Problem?" the chief interrupted.

"No problem." Alexis's hand moved unconsciously to the compass hanging around his neck. "Just catching up with old friends."

The chief's eyes narrowed, but Elena intervened. "Chief Dimitris, the equipment manifests need your signature here and here. For liability purposes."

The path to the monastery tested every suspension spring and frayed nerve. Each switchback peeled back more of the ancient structure while the harbor dropped away below.

Abbot Kyrillos stood at the gates in black robes untouched by the wind-blown dust coating everything else. His blue eyes tracked their approach without urgency, without surprise.

"Dr. Stavros. You return with an army."

"Hardly an army. Just qualified professionals with proper safety protocols."

"Ah, yes. Safety." The Abbot's gaze moved to each team member. "But who shall keep you safe from what you seek?"

Before Marcus could respond, Father Thomas stepped forward. "Father Abbot. The Vatican sends greetings."

"Rome takes interest in old stones?" The Abbot accepted the documents without reading them. "Or what lies beneath them?"

The monastery bells tolled at no canonical hour. Elena's equipment registered the sound frequencies and logged everything.

Brother Andreas led them through passages that looped back on themselves, corridors that shouldn't connect but did. The same courtyard appeared three times, each time from a different angle. Marcus tried to track their route and gave up. They always turned away before reaching the main chapel.

"Kitchen records," Andreas said too quickly when Marcus pointed this out. "Very boring."

Their base camp setup drew the local children like magnets. Quick hands traced protective symbols in the dust before scattering at Alexis's approach. He knelt to study one drawing. Rough lines. Something emerging from beneath the monastery.

Chief Dimitris appeared, brushing the drawing away with his foot. "Children's games. Nothing to concern yourselves with."

His hand shook as he pocketed the evidence.

As the sun set, Marcus noticed his shadow falling toward the monastery rather than away from it. Elena documented the phenomenon, though her voice cracked. "The photon behavior defies basic physics."

"Probably nothing. Instrument error."

But they all saw it.

That night, the equipment lit up with impossible data. Temperatures spiked and dropped in waves. Electromagnetic readings formed letters in ancient Greek before collapsing into noise. And underneath it all, the sensation of being watched by something that had been waiting a very long time.

"Standard atmospheric variations," Elena said. Her hands trembled as she logged readings no atmosphere had ever produced.

Chief Dimitris arrived with the dawn, now wearing a tactical vest and a larger sidearm than the day before. "There have been... incidents. Other research teams. Equipment failures. Accidents." He paused on that last word. "Perhaps you should reconsider."

The monastery bells interrupted him.

By dawn, the boats had returned to their moorings, but the strangeness remained. "The foundation shows micro-fractures consistent with extreme pressure," Elena reported, voice carefully neutral. "But the force originates from within the rock matrix itself."

The helicopter's rotors reached them first, soft and distant, then swelling until the sound devoured everything else. Victoria Nash emerged looking like someone who'd already been in motion before the call came in.

Chief Dimitris had phoned her that morning, as she'd instructed him to weeks ago. She'd been on the next flight out.

She walked toward them with questions already prepared, concern practiced to perfection. But she stopped short when she saw how they stood. Not scattered. Not arguing. Shoulder to shoulder, bodies angled to shield their equipment, their samples, everything they'd learned about what waited below.

"Perhaps we should discuss proper oversight," she said.

New shouts from the harbor cut her off. The anchored boats had broken free and formed an arrow pointing directly at the monastery.

The bells tolled. Elena's instruments shrieked. Sarah's dive watch stopped, the display showing only darkness. And Alexis's broken compass finally settled, pointing not north but in the same direction as the boats below.

"You see?" Abbot Kyrillos's voice carried over the chaos. "The old barriers weaken. What was bound seeks freedom. And you would break the seals that better men died maintaining."

Ethics board representatives crowded Victoria, voices rising. Chief Dimitris barked into his radio. But Marcus watched the shadows on the monastery wall creep sideways without any light to cast them, forming patterns that matched the warnings carved in stone.

They had until sunrise. The choice was simple. Proceed officially and fail, or wait for darkness and find another way in.

The monastery bells rang once more, deeper than before. In the harbor, the unmanned boats strained against their moorings.

Marcus gathered his team as twilight bled the color from the sky.

"Victoria's lockdown takes effect at sunrise," he said. "But the monastery has more than one entrance."

Elena spread her structural scans across the table. "There's an anomaly in the eastern wall. The stones show disturbance within the last week. Someone's already been inside."

"Brother Russo," Father Thomas said quietly. "The Abbot

mentioned him. Found his equipment but not him."

"Not him." Marcus traced a gap in the wall schematic. "Which means there's a way in he found. And if it's been used recently, it might still be open."

Sarah's hands moved over her equipment. "But we go prepared. Full safety protocols. Multiple exit routes."

"Agreed." Elena was already redistributing gear into portable configurations. "If we encounter what Russo encountered."

"We won't end up like him," Alexis said. His brother's compass had finally stopped its manic spinning, pointing steadily toward the eastern wall. "Whatever's down there, it's been calling specific people. People like us."

Maria looked up from her artifact documentation. "People with the right kind of damage. The right resonance." She touched her bandages without seeming to notice. "We're certainly compatible."

The word hung between them as darkness fell. One by one, they made their preparations. Equipment sorted, prayers spoken, escape routes memorized.

Chief Dimitris's patrols circled the perimeter, but Alexis knew the ruins, and he knew the man doing them. Island boys who'd grown up together, now playing different roles. He guided the team through shadows, past cameras, to where the eastern wall waited.

The entrance was exactly where Elena's scans had predicted. Stones shifted aside, recently, by a person or something else.

"Last chance to reconsider," Marcus said.

Nobody stopped.

Chapter 8

Their lights carved thin paths through the dark. The passage sloped down at an angle that burned Marcus's calves, and the floor was smooth, worn by water that had been here before. Maybe still was. The air tasted mineral and cold.

Marcus's flashlight swept the floor and caught something metallic. A camera, its lens shattered. Beside it, a leather pack, empty and torn. Brother Russo's gear was scattered like he'd dropped it without stopping.

Elena's equipment chirped and whined. Sarah counted steps under her breath. Father Thomas's prayer rope clicked against his belt with every stride. Alexis moved ahead like someone following a map only he could see.

The passage opened into a chamber that swallowed their light.

Elena's ground-penetrating radar made no sense. On her screen, the chambers shifted between scans, passages appearing in several configurations at once.

"This whole space is in flux." Her voice was flat, controlled. Her knuckles were white on the scanner. "Matter in multiple states simultaneously."

Father Thomas swept his flashlight across the wall they'd

entered through. The symbols seemed to rewrite themselves under the beam. The crucifix at his chest had gone cold.

Marcus pressed his palm against the stone where Elena's scans showed the instability. The wall rippled under his hand like something alive. The whole team stepped back at once, boots scraping stone. Nobody spoke. Nobody knew if what they'd seen was real or whether they'd all gone somewhere together that they couldn't come back from.

"My brother wrote about this," Alexis said, his eyes moving between the wall and the frantic notes in his hand. "Stone that remembers. Walls that learn."

The opening appeared not as a door but as something dissolving. Solid rock went permeable, a shimmering curtain of non-space that allowed passage without making sense. Sarah's instruments shrieked about pressure differentials that couldn't exist.

"We need to get the base camp established," Elena said, already running logistics for a structure that refused to obey physics. "If this passage closes…"

"We'll find another way," Marcus said. None of them believed him.

They passed through the stone one at a time. It parted like cold mercury. Solid matter flowed around them and through them, an intimacy the rock seemed to intend.

The space on the other side was wrong in every direction. Elena's instruments read 20 meters wide; her laser measure returned 200 meters from wall to wall at the same time. Fluted columns rose into darkness too deep for their lights to find a ceiling. The symbols on the columns hurt to look at directly, something about them catching at the corner of vision and refusing to resolve.

"Bioluminescent organisms," Sarah said, her voice thin. Her sensors found nothing.

They set up camp. Equipment placed against the east wall appeared minutes later against the west. Shadows fell the wrong way.

"The architecture is impossible," Elena muttered. "These support structures are bearing weight that doesn't exist, channeling force through..."

Her tablet flickered. Her data appeared briefly in ancient Greek, then came back.

Marcus had moved deeper, drawn to inscriptions that seemed to write themselves as he got close. "The script predates anything I know. But the patterns..." He traced the air without touching the stone. "Instructions. Or warnings. I can't tell yet."

The darkness shifted. Not an absence of light. Weight. Presence. Their headlamps dimmed together, batteries draining from something that wasn't in use.

"Stay together," Alexis said.

The walls moved. Flowed, really, slow and deliberate, and then there was no together to stay in.

Elena's world went silent between one breath and the next. Marcus was there, and then a wall of glowing stone had flowed between them, and he wasn't. The sounds of breathing, gear, boots, all of it gone. She was standing in nothing, alone with her scanner and the pale light.

"Marcus? Sarah?"

The quiet swallowed her voice without an echo.

Then the floor tilted.

It was slow at first. A nauseating list, like a ship finding its angle in heavy water. Her feet went light on one side, too heavy on the other, and then a loose pebble from her boot slid sideways, horizontally, and came to rest on the wall. The wall was the floor now. Gravity hadn't disappeared. It had simply decided to face a different direction.

She knew this feeling. She had felt it in Athens.

The same gentle sway, the same two or three seconds of wrongness before the main tremor hit. She had been standing in the parking garage when the concrete started to go, and she remembered understanding it exactly the way an engineer does… the load paths failing in sequence, the rebar losing its argument with physics, the building saying something that couldn't be unsaid. The light here was the same color as the emergency lights had been. The groan of stone around her now was the same sound.

She was back in the garage. She was also here. Both things were true, and neither helped.

"No." She raised her laser measure. Aimed at the new floor. Distance: 4.7 meters. Aimed at the ceiling. Distance: 4.7 meters. A perfect cube. Her instruments said she was fine. Her body said she was about to fall sideways into nothing. Her memory said she was already dead.

"Can anyone hear me?" Her voice came through the radio, muffled by static.

Elsewhere, Sarah stood in a chamber where water fell upward. Father Thomas knelt somewhere, his prayers came back in languages he'd never spoken. Alexis walked the paths his brother had left marked.

Marcus stayed in the center. Ancient text moved across the stone like something alive, and he stopped trying to understand it and just read *What sleeps below remembers the weight of mountains, the pressure of seas. It dreams of a time when darkness was ever-present, when the void was not empty but full.*

"The spaces are overlapping," Sarah said, her voice breaking up. "I'm flooded and dry at the same time. The water is in superposition until I…" Static.

They found each other again, as if the space were willing to allow it. They stood in a circle, backs to one another.

"It's not trying to hurt us," Maria said. She'd had more time with the artifact than any of them, and that gave her a kind of terrible vocabulary for this. "It's curious. The stone that attacked me was something like this, but this is older. It's taking its time."

"Taking its time doing what?" Sarah asked.

"This place is reading us," Elena said. Her voice was steadier now, which was worse somehow. "Biological signatures, psychological patterns. It found…"

"Our wounds," Father Thomas said. He didn't phrase it as a question.

The darkness pressed in, patient and interested. It had what it needed. Now it would see what to do with it.

"We go deeper," Marcus said. The words from the stone were still in him, still burning. "Whatever this is, it's further down."

"Down is relative," Elena said, watching her instruments place them simultaneously at sea level and a kilometer underground.

New passages appeared on her screen. Spirals through stone like corkscrews. Stairs that climbed and descended at the same time. Architecture meant for a geometry that their minds could only approximate.

The dark waited. It had waited a long time. These people were broken in exactly the right ways.

Chapter 9

The passage corkscrewed deeper, defying every attempt to map it. Sarah's compass spun without settling. Alexis's brother's notes had mentioned this descent, but the words hadn't made sense until now, *down becomes sideways becomes through.* The path didn't just go down. It went in directions without names.

The chamber opened without warning, vast and wrong. Water rose from the floor in a single column and spread across the ceiling in rivers that glowed with their own pale light.

"We're simultaneously at sea level and seven hundred meters below where we started." Sarah stopped, staring at her analyzer. "This can't be right."

"What is it?" Elena moved closer, her structural scanner tracking how the chamber reshaped itself around the water.

"It keeps shifting. Seawater one second, fresh the next, then something that isn't H2O at all but still acts like it." Sarah's fingers moved across her gear.

Marcus stood watching the patterns emerge in the rising liquid. The symbols matched those from the monastery foundations, but written in three dimensions, suspended in glowing water.

"Look at how the droplets arrange themselves," Father

Thomas said quietly, pointing to hovering spheres that formed geometries before dissolving. "Like a language being spoken in water."

The liquid reached their knees, then stopped.

The surface went still.

"It's waiting, I think," Alexis said. He recognized the patience from his brother's notes.

Elena's readings spiked. "Massive electromagnetic buildup. If this follows the same pattern as my earthquake data—"

The water erupted. Liquid tendrils rose fast, reaching for each of them with a precision that didn't feel random. Sarah's training took over. But this water didn't behave like any environment she'd trained for.

"Don't resist," she called out. "It's not attacking. It's watching us."

A tendril wrapped around her wrist, and she was somewhere else. Still in the chamber, but also standing in the cave system off Crete, watching David's light descend into darkness. The water showed her what she had never seen. His final moments, the thing he found that made him choose depth over surface.

"He wasn't lost," she said. "He chose to go deeper."

The vision broke apart when Father Thomas began to pray. His Latin made the water recoil, then gather again with different intent. It showed him a flooded cathedral, holy water climbing stone pillars, baptismal fonts opening onto vast underwater spaces.

Each of them saw something the others didn't. Elena watched water move through gaps in solid rock so small they shouldn't have existed, and for a moment she felt close to understanding something she couldn't quite hold. Alexis saw his brother move through flooded caves that existed between known places. Marcus read texts written in liquid motion, words that dissolved before he could translate them.

"It's alive," Maria said, watching the water shape itself into the artifacts she'd spent years studying. "I don't know how. But it remembers."

The water began pulling back. It compressed without losing volume, leaving pockets of space behind that had no right to be there. Sarah's instruments stopped trying to rationalize the readings. Error messages appeared on her screens in languages that predated the machines.

When the water was gone, they stood changed in ways none of them had words for. Damp but not wet. They had breathed underwater without drowning.

"There's more below," Marcus said. The old words were still moving through him like something that didn't want to stop. "This was just the beginning."

"That's where my brother went," Alexis said. "Where David went. I think that's where this whole place makes sense."

Sarah checked her dive watch. It was showing her moments that hadn't happened yet, depths measured in potential rather than distance. "The water is connecting everything. Each space we find."

"Theologically speaking," Father Thomas said, his rosary still dripping water that had no business existing, "what we just went through was something like a baptism. In the loosest sense of the word."

Elena's scanner showed the chamber had changed. Passages had opened where solid stone had been minutes before, following the lines the water had traced.

"We need to document this," Maria said, but her cameras showed only empty rock. The water had refused to be recorded,

61

just as the artifacts that came after her had refused to leave any evidence. Real, while it happened, impossible to prove.

"Then we keep going," Marcus said.

The new passages spiraled down through angles that couldn't be charted, moving through some concept of depth their minds could only approximate. Sarah led, her diving instincts adjusting to spaces that were neither fully liquid nor entirely solid.

Behind them, the chamber sealed itself. Stone shifted like water, removing every trace of their passage. Ahead, other things waited. The sound of water moving through spaces that couldn't hold it. The smell of seas that had never seen sunlight. A pressure that felt less like depth and more like age.

"Whatever's down there," Sarah said, watching her instruments flicker, "it's been waiting. The water was just its way of getting us ready."

She stopped.

They had come out onto a ledge overlooking something that wasn't a cave or a chamber. It was an interior ocean. The water was black, very still, and very old. Bioluminescence moved through it in slow patterns, spelling out warnings in languages they were only beginning to recognize.

Sarah's watch kept ticking, counting down to something it couldn't name. Around them the stone went on changing, learning something from the water that had passed through it, solid shifting toward something else entirely.

Chapter 10

The passage ended not at a wall but at a threshold. Before them stood a single massive door of seamless, unearthly bronze. Its surface was layered with inscriptions written over one another for millennia, warnings stacked atop warnings until they blurred into something like geology.

"No oxidation," Elena said quietly. Her laser measure swept across the surface, its readings flickering. "After centuries, it should show patina, corrosion. But it's pristine."

Father Thomas leaned closer, his rosary beads clicking softly against the cold metal. "These passages... I don't recognize them. Not Greek, not any ancient language I know. It's as if someone was trying to write about something language couldn't hold." The symbols beneath his fingers seemed to shift, moving away from his touch. He found a deeper layer, a script that made his blood run cold.

The central lock mechanism was an intricate maze of interlocking circles, each ring inscribed with symbols that pulsed faintly. Marcus reached toward it without deciding to. The bronze around the lock liquified and shaped itself into words *Here lies the threshold between what is and what hungers to be.*

He stared at them. His pulse climbed, not with fear but with something closer to relief. This was what he'd spent his entire life looking for. Every failed theory, every mocked presentation, every sleepless night. It had all been leading here.

I need to understand. The need burned through him until his hands shook. *I need to see what's beyond.*

The bronze rippled.

The lock responded. Not to his touch, not to any physical key, but to something it recognized in him. The interlocking circles began to rotate, clicking into alignment with a sound like bones settling. Each ring turned to match something. He didn't have a word for what. The shape of thirty years of obsession, maybe. A need so consuming that it had cost him everything, and he still wasn't satisfied.

Before his fingers made contact, the lock clicked open. The sound moved through the cave and kept going, resonating somewhere past the walls. The door swung inward on hinges that made no sound despite their weight.

The room beyond was a vast library. Like everything else they'd found, it refused to match the mapping data.

The smell hit them first. Papyrus and leather. "This can't exist," Elena breathed. Her equipment put the room at three hundred meters in every direction. "We're inside solid bedrock."

"Look at the preservation." Maria had already moved toward the nearest shelf, her voice a conservator's mix of awe and dread. "Perfect temperature. Perfect humidity. These texts should have crumbled to dust centuries ago."

The shelves rose beyond the reach of their lights. Books lined every surface, bound in strange leathers. Scrolls of hammered metal, their surfaces etched with harsh, deliberate marks. Some volumes held no text at all, only shadows and images pressed somehow into the pages.

Father Thomas approached one shelf slowly. "These are theological texts," he said, "but inverted. Prayers to different gods. Liturgies for ceremonies that celebrate decay." He pulled his hand back. "This knowledge isn't right. It's a poison."

"Then why preserve it?" Elena asked. She was documenting the architecture in her notebook, trying not to look at the way it folded in on itself.

It was Alexis who found the answer. He'd been watching the shelves, not the books. "It's not preservation," he said. "It's imprisonment. The carvings on the walls aren't decorative. They're binding runes. Each text is a captured piece of something."

The whispers started before he finished the sentence.

Every book and scroll began to vibrate in a low, harmonious drone. The air grew heavy. Then the sound stopped, all at once.

In the silence, they heard breathing. Slow and patient.

"What the hell is that?" Elena whispered.

Marcus moved between the stacks without deciding to. His feet carried him forward, his pulse climbing with each step. The shelves opened before him, one gap after another. Behind him, the others hurried to keep up.

The stacks opened into a circular chamber.

A pedestal of polished black stone rose from the floor at the center. Above it, a shaft cut through the ceiling, but no light came down through it. On the pedestal sat a box, black as the stone beneath it. The air around it looked wrong, somehow dimmer, as if something pulled at the edges of the torchlight.

Marcus reached out. His fingers stopped inches from the surface. His hands shook. Not from fear. He knew this box. He had never seen it before. He grasped the lid and lifted.

Sound erupted from the gap, sharp and vast, like air rushing into a space that had never held breath. Marcus flinched but didn't let go. Inside lay a single scroll. The material wasn't parchment or paper. It looked like a strip of night sky torn free, black and depthless. Characters marked its surface, pale and slightly luminous.

He read without knowing the language but understood it. *Written before light was separated from the dark.*

He lifted the scroll. It throbbed faintly, syncing to his pulse. The text shimmered, and he began to read aloud, the words coming out in fluent ancient Greek. A language he knew. Not like this.

"Before light, darkness reigned absolute. A sentient void, older than all living things. The Greeks called it Erebus. But it was ancient even before the first sound was imagined."

Black liquid welled up from beneath the scroll. It spread across the pedestal in lines that branched, folded, twisted back. Father Thomas raised his hand. His fingers traced the sign of the cross. No prayer followed.

Marcus kept reading. The words weren't quite his anymore. Deeper, older, coming from somewhere he couldn't locate. "When Nyx, the Night, first embraced Erebus, their union gave shape to the first laws of reality. The night sky with its stars. Dreams to bring hope. Nightmares for despair. And fate for all living things." He paused. "But their love was a devouring one. Erebus's hunger turned inward on his own children."

"Marcus." Sarah's voice was thin and flat. Her knuckles had gone white around the scanner. "The cave's changing. The markings on the pedestal." She tilted the screen toward the light. "They're a map."

Elena stepped closer. "A map of what?"

Sarah's lips moved. No sound came out. She tried again. "I'm not sure."

The scroll shifted in his hands. He kept reading. "Nyx, unable to destroy her lover, tore Erebus apart, scattering its fragments across reality, binding each piece to a vessel that could contain its hunger."

Father Thomas stared at the branching lines. "Each chamber in the diagram is a different fragment." His voice had dropped almost to nothing. "We're standing in the record of how a goddess dismantled her love to save everything else."

The scroll pulsed. Heat spread through Marcus's palms. His voice cracked. "The vessels were chosen with terrible care. Souls marked by specific darkness, their wounds shaped to match the fragments they must hold. Through their wounds the Night would bind her love, until time itself grows dark and cold."

Marcus's fingers tightened.

The library screamed.

Not with sound. Pressure built in their chests and skulls instead, sudden and enormous. Every book vibrated at once. Sarah's scanner shattered in her hands. Elena stumbled, palms pressed to her temples. Father Thomas dropped to one knee.

Marcus stood rigid, eyes rolling back. Knowledge poured through him, too fast, too much, with nowhere to go.

Alexis grabbed his arm and pulled him away from the pedestal. Marcus gasped and nearly went down. Blood ran from his nose in bright lines.

"We're not investigators." The words came out between ragged breaths. "We're containers. Vessels."

The darkness between the shelves began to move. Not drifting. Moving toward something. Text lifted from pages, black ink rising and flowing through the air. The streams circled them, patient and deliberate.

A voice rose from everywhere at once. Paper rustling. A million pages turning together. Words formed from the sound, pressing against their skin.

WHAT WAS BOUND STILL DREAMS. WHAT WAS SCATTERED SEEKS REUNION. WHAT WAS BROKEN RECOGNIZES ITS VESSELS.

"Run." Marcus's voice cut through the noise.

They ran.

The passages bent around them. Shelves slid past too quickly or opened ahead of them. Behind them, pages rustled. Whispers moved through the aisles. Shadows pooled beneath the shelves, thick and patient.

Marcus's head throbbed. The knowledge coiled inside his skull, deeper with each heartbeat. He knew, with a certainty that turned his stomach, that they would come back. Not because they'd want to. Because the need would grow until it crowded out everything else, and returning would feel like the only thing that made sense.

Chapter 11

They stumbled into the next chamber and stopped.

No books. No shelves. Just smooth stone rising into shadow. The air pressed down, cold and still. It felt old. It felt like it was watching.

The knowledge from the library hadn't left. It sat heavy in Marcus's chest, coiled around his thoughts. Everything they'd seen now meant something different.

His boot scraped against stone. A scroll lay at the chamber's center, small and tightly rolled. He knelt, worked the binding loose, and the scroll unrolled across the cold floor. The characters moved at the edges of his vision, twisting, never quite holding still.

Elena fumbled with her equipment. Her hands shook. She'd calibrated instruments in cramped dig sites, fingers steady in freezing mountain passes. Now they wouldn't obey. Architectural diagrams appeared on the flickering screen, lines folding into impossible angles that should have meant nothing. But they did. The deeper they went, the more she understood. Her instruments told her less than her own eyes now.

Marcus looked up from the scroll. His eyes had gone empty. "For us."

He pulled in a breath that scraped. The words came out harsh, dragged from somewhere deep.

"The binding… the original binding was a thing of force, of stone and ritual. But it was imperfect. It could weaken. A new binding requires something more intimate. Vessels, prepared by specific trauma, whose wounds create a perfect resonance with the fragments they must contain."

Then the chamber began to change.

Shadows pooled in the corners, thick and black. They didn't spread. They gathered with purpose, peeling away from the walls one by one, moving against the torchlight, against reason. Smoke that held weight. Darkness given form.

One drifted toward Father Thomas.

He went rigid. His breath stopped. The rosary beads slipped through his fingers. The shadow stretched, thinned, shaped itself. A hand. Slender fingers reaching through the dark, the same fingers he'd last seen through smoke and flames.

Maria's hand.

"Maria." The name tore out of him like something physical.

His fingers found the beads again. Click. Click. Click. Faster. Frantic. He clamped his eyes shut, and the Latin poured out. "Pater noster, qui es in caelis…"

The words fell flat. Dead in the air. From the darkness came an echo, his own prayer but wrong. The voice beneath it was older than speech, twisting the syllables into something that wanted.

The shadow hand reached. Fingers brushed his cheek.

Cold flooded through him. Not the absence of warmth but a presence, something alive. It drank the heat from his skin, burrowed into bone, pulled at something deeper than flesh.

Then the smell hit him. Burning wood. Melting plastic. Smoke thick in his throat. He wasn't in the cave anymore.

He was ten years old again. Standing in the hallway. Maria's door on his left. The stairs to safety on his right. The choice before him, terrible and alive, burning hotter than the flames.

"Tom?" The whisper came from the shadow, and it was her voice, perfect and unbroken by time. "Why did you leave me?"

"No." He stumbled back. "This isn't real."

The rosary burned in his hand. He couldn't let go. The wooden beads shifted and rearranged themselves. The cross at the end twisted slowly, turning upside down. The familiar loop of prayer broke apart into shapes he didn't recognize. Angles that hurt to look at. The monastery's symbols, carved into his faith like a knife into wood.

Marcus's voice cut through the chamber. Still reading, still translating the scroll's writhing text. "Through their broken places shall the Ancient Dark remember itself, rising through channels carved in mortal pain."

The shadows multiplied.

They poured from every corner, spreading across the floor, climbing the walls. Elena heard the crack first. A sharp snap of stone splitting. She looked up. The smooth walls fractured, lines spreading like veins. Then came the sound beneath it. A groan. High-pitched. Metal screaming as it bent, stretched, and tore past what it could bear.

She knew that sound.

Her legs went weak. The cave vanished. She was in the parking garage in Athens. Three floors underground. Concrete dust thick in her lungs. Emergency lights cast everything in a sickly blue glow. The ceiling sagged. Rebar shrieked. She had seconds.

"It's a manifestation." Her voice shook. She forced the words out, clinging to them. "It's using our memories as a template."

71

But the floor beneath her began to shake. That rhythm. She'd felt it before. The support columns buckled in sequence.

She stared at the cracks spreading across the stone. They formed paths. Channels. The darkness flowed through them, following principles she'd spent years studying. Structural failure points. Load distribution. Stress fractures. The cave wasn't just replaying her trauma. It was showing her that Athens hadn't been random. It had been engineered.

Marcus choked on the next line. "The fragments recognize each other. Through mortal vessels shall scattered pieces remember their whole." He snapped back, eyes showing color again.

They turned to run. The passage behind them rippled. The walls sealed together with the slow finality of a closing door.

"Fall back to the center," Marcus shouted.

The stone beneath their feet flowed like molten glass, reshaping itself into spirals and glyphs that pulsed with dark light.

"The binding must be failing." Elena watched the patterns crawl up her boots, spreading across all of their hands. "The fragments aren't just trying to reunite. They're doing it through us. Erebus is rebuilding itself through us."

The darkness pressed in. No more testing. No more patience. It came with the weight of gravity, mapping itself onto each of them. It knew exactly where to go.

For Marcus, it coiled into the vast emptiness in his gut. The space where his hunger lived, where knowledge and redemption had twisted together until he couldn't separate them.

For Elena, it flowed into the fault lines of her guilt. Cold pressure solidified in her mind. She felt the rubble. The weight of the earth around her.

For Father Thomas, it slid into the hollow his betrayal had carved. The piece of himself he'd lost in the fire was returning, black and cold.

For Alexis, it filled the endless corridors of his grief. The deep sinking feeling of being completely alone.

For Sarah, it surged into the drowning silence. Her lungs remembered water. Cold. Heavy. The sensation didn't stop.

Sarah gasped. The gasp became a choke. Her hands flew to her throat, clawing at nothing. No air came. Only water.

Clear and cold, it poured from her lips. Impossible. Real. Splashing onto stone in streams that shouldn't exist.

"Sarah!" Marcus lunged.

She staggered back, eyes bulging. Her chest heaved. Drowning on dry land. The sound was wet, desperate, the horrible music of lungs filling with liquid instead of air.

Elena grabbed her shoulders and tried to turn her. Sarah's body convulsed. Her skin drained of color. Blue spread across her lips. The water kept coming, pooling around their feet, spreading in widening circles.

Father Thomas reached for her. His hands met something cold. The shadow inside Sarah wasn't just occupying her trauma. It was finishing it, completing what the lake had started years ago.

Sarah's eyes found theirs. Wide with terror. Pleading.

She collapsed.

The water stopped. Her body struck stone. The pool began to rise as mist, pulling back into whatever had birthed it.

The cave understood what happened next before any of them did.

From Sarah's open, staring eyes, a tendril of absolute darkness emerged. Not the black of night. The black of the void. The absence of light, of hope. It moved with the fluid grace of water, the weight of something that had been waiting a long time.

"The fragment," Father Thomas breathed. "It's transferring."

The dark tendril reached for Marcus. It wasn't attacking. It recognized him as the axis, the center point around which everything else would orbit. Sarah's piece had learned the shape of her drowning. Now it carried that knowledge toward its final vessel.

Marcus tried to pull back. His body wouldn't obey. Some deeper part of him, the part that had always needed to possess every truth, reached out instead.

When the fragment touched his chest, he convulsed. The sensation was drowning in air, his lungs filling with darkness. He felt Sarah's final moments. The pressure of seven hundred meters. The cold so complete it stopped thought. The terrible peace of giving in.

But underneath that, something else. Her determination. Her scientific precision even in the face of the impossible. Her love of the truth hidden in dark places. The strengths that had made her compatible with the fragment in the first place. Now they were his.

"Four fragments," Elena said, her voice shaking. "Four wounds. But now all four are converging on one vessel."

"The binding is adapting," Alexis said. His brother's compass spun in his pocket. "It was supposed to be distributed. Four people, four prisons. But if one vessel can be made strong enough…"

"Then the binding becomes absolute," Father Thomas finished. "Not scattered across four souls but concentrated in one. Unbreakable. No weak link. No chain to break."

Marcus gasped as the fragment settled into him. His body

began to glow from within, dark light pulsing through his veins. "Sarah's death wasn't a failure." His voice already carried harmonics that weren't entirely human. "It was the binding optimizing itself."

The cave pulsed in affirmation. A deep, satisfied throb.

"We're not the four vessels anymore," Elena said. "We're the three witnesses. And Marcus is becoming the prison."

The implications settled over them quietly, the way bad news does when you've already suspected it. The fragments from each of them would still be torn free. Elena's guilt, Thomas's betrayal, Alexis's grief. But they wouldn't hold those fragments forever. They'd feed them all to Marcus, whose obsession was deep enough, old enough, to contain all of Erebus.

Sarah's sacrifice hadn't broken the ritual. It had finished it.

Marcus looked at Sarah's empty body, at the pool of water that held the memory of her shape. "I'm sorry," he whispered. Whether he was apologizing to her or for her, none of them could say.

The darkness receded completely within him, and the transformation accelerated.

Marcus dropped to his knees. Pressed his fingers to her neck. Nothing. Her chest was still. Eyes open, staring at the ceiling. A film of moisture glazed them.

"No." Alexis's whisper cracked. "No, no, no…"

But the binding didn't stop. The darkness had taken its fill of Sarah. It moved on. Patient. Ready for the next vessel.

"We can still make a run for it!" Father Thomas said, and even he heard the lie.

They had been marked since birth. Shaped through trauma into perfect vessels for something that had waited since before time began.

The library pulsed, calling them back. A massive heartbeat that reverberated toward them. They could feel the fragments of Erebus stirring inside themselves, in the broken places that had always belonged to something older than human sorrow.

"Then we face it together." Elena's voice surprised her with its steadiness. "Whatever we're becoming, don't let it take us one by one. Not like Nicolas. Not like Sarah."

They pressed their backs together, forming a circle. Small and fragile in the encroaching dark. But even united, they felt it. Their traumas had become doorways, and something vast was already beginning to crawl through.

The transformation had already begun. The darkness didn't need to shatter walls or breach defenses. It had shaped them into keys long before they'd ever arrived at the lock.

Far below, something vast shifted. The chains trembled, slackening with every beat of their hearts.

The darkness closed in, steady and sure.

Then it released them.

The pressure vanished. The shadows retreated, flowing back into the walls like water draining from a basin. The chamber's geometry snapped into place, solid and comprehensible again. The way forward was clear.

Marcus staggered first. His legs moved without his permission, carrying him toward the exit. "No." He dug his heels in. His body kept walking. "No, I'm not…"

The others followed. One by one, their feet betrayed them. Elena reached for the wall and her hand slid past. Father Thomas's rosary clattered to the ground as he lurched forward, leaving it behind.

They weren't running. They were being pulled. An invisible current swept them through the passages, around corners, up slopes. The monastery's depths released them the way a tide releases driftwood, gentle and inexorable. Their equipment dragged behind them, forgotten. Their protests died in their throats.

The cave mouth appeared ahead. Moonlight spilled across the entrance, pale and cold. They stumbled into the open air, gasping, and the pulling stopped.

Their campsite lay before them. Tents still standing. Gear arranged exactly as they'd left it. The fire pit held gray ash, long cold.

Marcus collapsed to his knees and pressed his hands into the dirt. Solid. Real. The others stood in stunned silence, staring back at the cave entrance.

It had let them go.

But the fragments were still there, nested in their broken places, quiet and patient. And somewhere far below, the chains were a little looser than they'd been before.

Chapter 12

The camp offered no comfort. Packs formed a rough circle, gaps between them barely wide enough to pass through. No one had discussed it. They'd arranged it that way, each person creating a barrier against something that was already inside their heads.

Marcus paced. Back and forth. Back and forth. His boots scraped against stone that glittered with a thousand tiny reflections, watching him. He'd spread Elena's scans across a flat rock, the images casting a sickly glow.

"The implications are staggering." His voice thrummed low and intense, vibrating with something that wasn't quite his anymore. "If the cave can manifest physical matter from psychological imprints, it means consciousness is a tangible force here."

Elena sat hunched in the corner, a thermal blanket tight around her shoulders. She clutched Sarah's old diving watch to her chest. Her knuckles had gone white. Her whole body shook.

Marcus didn't notice. Or couldn't stop himself from talking.

"Why did it release us?" He spun toward the cave entrance, eyes wild. "We were there. The binding was starting. The fragments recognized us." His hands clenched into fists. "Why pull us back? Why show us everything and then just... let us go?"

He kicked at a loose stone. It skittered across the camp and disappeared into the shadows.

"It doesn't make sense. None of this makes sense." But even as he said it, frustration cracked his voice. Because it did make sense. Some part of him understood. The part that wasn't entirely his anymore. "Unless... unless it's not done preparing us."

The thought settled over him like ice water. His pacing stopped.

They weren't released out of mercy. They were released the way a farmer releases livestock into a pasture. To fatten. To ripen. The binding wasn't ready yet, but it would be. And when it was, the cave would call them back. They'd walk down into the dark again, and this time there would be no returning.

"I need to check the structural integrity," Elena said, her voice thin and artificially calm, a desperate attempt to impose the logic of her profession on what was happening around her. Her fingers fumbled with the medical kit, spilling sterile gauze and ampules across the dusty floor. "Heart rates are elevated across the board. We're all showing signs of extreme physiological stress."

"Whatever is going on here, we've stumbled onto something incredible. And if this site is anything like the others, we connected the signs to, it proves everything!" Marcus's words tumbled over hers, a torrent of obsessive discovery. "The pre-Christian sites, the connection between architecture and consciousness, the geometric patterns as a form of living language..."

A single dark trickle of blood ran from his left nostril. He wiped it away with the back of his hand, leaving a red smear across his cheek. He didn't seem to notice.

Father Thomas crossed to Elena's side. His face had gone pale, slick with sweat. He moved slowly, deliberately, pressing a water bottle into her shaking hands. When he knelt to help gather the scattered supplies, they both froze. His movements were too smooth. Too steady. The hand reaching for bandages didn't belong to a man crushed by guilt. It belonged to something that had learned to wear his skin.

"We should stop." His voice came out low, pleading. "We need to find a way out."

Behind him, shadows writhed along the cave wall. They formed shapes he recognized. A window frame. The curve of a young girl's shoulder. Maria, reaching for him through the dark. He jerked away, breath hitching. Marcus didn't look up, still lost in his theorizing.

"Don't you see? The manifestations are tailored with surgical precision to…"

"To kill us," Alexis said quietly from the edge of their small circle of light. Since the water chamber had taken Sarah, he'd positioned himself as their watchman. His eyes never stopped moving, scanning the darkness, searching for the patterns that had claimed his brother. "Like it killed her."

Sarah's name landed between them like a stone dropped in still water. The ripples spread, silent and heavy. Her absence carved a hole in their formation. Every impossible thing they encountered now, they faced without her expertise. An amputated limb they felt with phantom pain.

Her equipment lay scattered among them. Alexis wore her backup scanner on his belt. Elena had clipped Sarah's altimeter to her pack. Each piece a reminder. Knowledge had a price in this place. They were still paying it.

Elena's tablet flickered. The screen was washed with light, but no data appeared. Instead, images bled across the display. A concrete pillar buckling, dust billowing. A child's hand reaching through smoke. A compass needle spinning, never settling. Her own nightmare. Thomas's. Alexis's. Pulled from their minds and displayed like specimens.

She flinched but kept typing. Her fingers moved with clinical precision, each keystroke an act of defiance. She documented everything. The anomalies. Their symptoms. Their collective unraveling. A scientist cataloging the death of reason itself.

"We need to discuss extraction." Father Thomas's voice cut through Marcus's rambling. A single drop of blood appeared at his hairline, sliding toward his temple. "These symptoms, Marcus. They are not just side effects. They are a process."

"They are revolutionary!" Marcus pulled up more images, hands trembling. Fever or excitement, impossible to say. "If we can document this process, understand the mechanism by which the cave accesses and manifests these memories..."

Static burst from his radio.

The crackle resolved into voices. Clear. Distinct. A child crying. "Mama? Mama, where are you?" Elena's voice. Young. Terrified. Aftershock debris was settling around her.

Then prayers in a teenage boy's broken whisper. "Please, God. Please. Take it back. Undo it. Please." Thomas, years ago, kneeling in ash and smoke.

Rain hammering. A man's voice raw from screaming. "Nicolas! Nicolas!" Over and over. Alexis, searching in the dark.

Their past selves played on loop. The cave sampled their pain, tasting each moment, savoring it.

"It's studying us." Elena stared at her equipment. Their

vital signs pulsed on the screen, synchronizing. Not with each other. With something else. A rhythm rising from deep below. Vast. Slow. Patient. "It's learning which wounds cut deepest. Learning the shape of us."

Marcus spun toward her. His eyes blazed with manic intensity. "Then we study it back! This is what I have worked for my entire life! Proof that consciousness can shape reality, that ancient sites were built to channel and amplify psychic energy..."

"Your nose." Father Thomas's voice cut sharply with alarm.

Marcus touched his cheek, annoyed at the interruption. His fingers came away wet. Dark red. Not a trickle anymore. Blood ran freely down his jaw, but his eyes didn't follow it. They stared past his hand, unblinking, fixed on something in the darkness only he could see.

Behind him, the shadows thickened. Gathered. A shape formed. A woman's silhouette. Her head tilted, eyes glinting with something between pity and triumph.

Victoria Nash.

The cave wall rippled. Chairs materialized in silent rows, their worn velvet seats drinking the light. The smell of old paper and dust filled the air. Pages fluttered down the walls like snow. Rejection letters. Critical reviews. Notices of censure. They overlapped, layer upon layer, until stone disappeared beneath a suffocating skin of failure.

"Minor hemorrhaging is expected with sudden and extreme pressure changes." Marcus's voice shifted, taking on a lecturing tone. Distant. Academic. "The important thing is to document the phenomena."

Elena's equipment shrieked. A single piercing note, then the screen went black. The world tilted. Vertigo slammed into her like a wave. Her knees buckled.

Father Thomas caught her before she hit the ground. His own balance wavered, feet shuffling to stay upright.

"The electromagnetic buildup is off the scale." She gasped the words out, head spinning. "If these patterns match what happened in the moments before Sarah…"

"We proceed." Marcus's voice boomed too loudly in the confined space, echoing off the stone. "This is exactly what they said was impossible! What Victoria said was nothing more than fringe fantasy!"

He stumbled. Swayed. His feet planted wide to keep himself standing. For a moment, the manic fire in his eyes died. Something else looked out from behind them. Ancient. Hungry. Still as deep water.

"Marcus?" Alexis stepped forward, hand drifting toward the knife at his belt.

"I'm fine." The words belonged to Marcus. The voice didn't. Not quite. Blood ran freely now, twin streams from both nostrils dripping off his chin onto the stone. "Better than fine. I can feel it. The knowledge, waiting below. Everything I theorized, everything they mocked me for…"

The lecture hall materialized behind him. Fully formed. Every detail precise. Rows of seats filled with shapes. Not people. Things that had once been people. Gaunt forms hunched in chairs, their edges blurred and indistinct. Eyes like tarnished coins, hollow and lightless. They watched in absolute silence. No breathing. No blinking. The ghosts of academia. His peers. Judging him. Weighing the obsessive fire in his chest against the eternal emptiness in their own.

"We have to leave." Elena forced the words out. Standing took everything she had. "The structural readings show massive instability. If we don't leave now…"

"Then go!"

The word exploded from Marcus's throat. But it wasn't just his voice. Layers beneath it. Harmonics no human vocal cords could produce. The sound reverberated through the chamber. Stone vibrated in response.

"Run back to your safety! Run back to your ignorance! I am going deeper."

He grabbed his pack. His limbs jerked and twitched, movements wrong, disjointed. Strings pulling a puppet. The others stood frozen, watching him. He didn't speak again. Didn't need to. Whatever moved inside his skin now wasn't the man they'd followed through storms and silence.

"The cave's presence is in his head." Father Thomas whispered, hand trembling as he crossed himself. "It found the engine that drives him and poured fuel on the fire."

Marcus stopped at the mouth of a newly formed passage. He looked back. The light caught his eyes wrong. Too sharp. Too bright. Like obsidian chips pressed into flesh. "Coming?"

Not a question. A command.

One by one, they followed. Silence closed around them, thick as held breath. The cave leaned in. Listening.

Blood dripped from Marcus's nose. Steady. Rhythmic as a metronome. Dark red dots marked the stone floor. He didn't wipe it away. With every step, the air grew heavier, dense with purpose.

Behind them, darkness crept closer. Shapes shifted at the edges of their vision.

Something had been started.

And it was hungry.

The chamber expelled them with the same inexorable force that had pulled them down, but this time they carried an immense weight.

Sarah's body had changed. The water that killed her had transformed her into something between flesh and the cave's own substance. Her skin held a faint, pearlescent sheen. When they tried to lift her, she felt both impossibly heavy and weightless at once, as if she existed in multiple states simultaneously.

"We can't leave her," Elena said, her voice breaking. She knelt beside Sarah's still form, one hand hovering over her colleague's cold cheek.

"The cave won't let us," Alexis replied, and he was right. Every time they tried to carry Sarah toward the passage leading up, their hands passed through her as if she were made of mist. Yet when they stopped trying, she was solid again. Undeniably real. Undeniably dead.

Marcus understood first. "She's part of it now," he said quietly. Blood still trickled from his nose. "The binding took her completely. Her body... it belongs to the depths."

Father Thomas began the last rites, his voice steady despite the tremor in his hands. The Latin echoed strangely in the chamber. As he spoke the final words, Sarah's form began to dissolve. Not decay. Dissolve. Like watercolor paint meeting water, her edges softened and spread, seeping into the stone floor in rivulets of luminescent liquid.

Elena reached out instinctively, but her fingers found only

cool stone.

"The water took her down there," Marcus continued. His voice was distant, already changing. "Now she is the water. Part of the system. Part of what we're here to contain."

Where Sarah's body had lain, a pattern remained in the stone. A network of delicate crystalline veins pulsed with faint bioluminescence, like the mineral deposits they'd seen in the water chamber but arranged with a deliberateness that made Elena's stomach turn.

"We tell them she was lost in the collapse," Elena said firmly, standing. "Buried. Unrecoverable. It's not a lie."

They stood there a moment longer. Then the cave pressed at their backs, and they had no choice but to go.

Marcus began to whistle as he walked. It was a jagged, tuneless thing that echoed off the stone, a melody of broken thirds and dissonant fifths. Not a song. Something older. A frequency that seemed to settle in the bones rather than the ear, threaded with something like hunger.

The others followed behind him. One by one, their thoughts began to blur at the edges. None of them noticed when their steps fell into rhythm with his.

The tune was catching.

And it was only just beginning.

Chapter 13

The limestone walls rippled. Slow and fleshy, like something massive drawing breath in its sleep. Father Thomas stood at the center, hand moving through the air, tracing half-remembered patterns. Latin spilled from his lips. The rites of exorcism. But the words twisted as they left his mouth, warping, rotting. The room ate his prayers. Each syllable stretched and thinned, drowning in invisible depths.

Color flickered against grey stone. Faint. A pattern forming where none should exist.

Yellow wallpaper bled through the rock.

His rosary slipped from his fingers. Thirty years of desperate prayer worn into the smooth beads. It hit the floor with a sharp clatter.

Maria's bedroom surrounded him.

Every detail was perfect. The pencils on her desk lined up in obsessive precision, sharpened to needle points. Her algebra homework lay half-finished, gentle looping curves frozen mid-equation. Their grandmother's silver rosary hung from the white bedpost, swinging slightly, as if someone had just brushed past. The air carried lavender and old books. A scent he'd spent a lifetime trying to forget.

Glass shattered below. The spiderweb crack of the back

door's window. A sound carved into the deepest part of his soul.

Father Thomas's heart stopped.

"Not again." His voice tore out raw and broken. "Not this. Anything but this."

But the past had already taken hold.

Light and memory formed a shape in the doorway. A boy. Gangly. Frightened. A threadbare Cubs jersey hung loose on thin shoulders. One foot hovered near Maria's door. The other pulled back toward the hallway, toward his own room, toward safety. The boy froze. Heavy boots thundered up the stairs. Raw panic flashed across his face.

He turned and fled silently. Desperate.

Thomas had watched this retreat in his nightmares for thirty years.

He looked down. Two sets of rosary beads filled his grip. One smooth, familiar wood from the present. The other cheap plastic from that night. Both wept slow tears. Thick. Crimson.

"Tom?" Maria's voice drifted from the bed. Young. Laced with fear that pierced straight through him. "Is somebody downstairs?"

Thomas watched, helpless, a prisoner trapped in his own private hell. His teenage self-pressed against the hallway wall, face twisted with indecision. The boy's lips moved. A silent prayer. The same prayer Thomas had recited every night for thirty years. Penance that never brought absolution.

"We have to help her!" Elena lunged for the door.

Her body passed through like smoke. Her hands met cold stone where the wooden frame should have been.

The intruders climbed the stairs. Shadows given physical form. Darkness was moving through two times at once.

Thomas tried to speak. To scream. To change the past through sheer force of will. But past and present tangled in his throat, choking him.

He looked down. His white clerical collar had turned the color of dried blood.

"The electromagnetic readings are off the scale." Elena's voice cut through, a desperate anchor to fracturing reality. "Whatever's happening, it's affecting fundamental forces."

The room flickered between states. Soft yellow bedroom. Cold grey cave. Dark, oppressive wood of a confessional booth. Through it all, Maria's voice. Threading through everything. Pulling at him.

"Tom? I can hear them on the stairs. Please! I'm scared!"

Both versions of Thomas stood frozen. The terrified boy who would choose survival. The broken priest who carried the weight of that choice. The rosaries pulsed in his hands with impossible, searing heat. Past and present. Sin and penance. Trying to occupy the same space at the same time.

Then a new voice spoke.

"I forgive you."

The words came from nowhere and everywhere. Not Maria's voice as it had been, young and frightened. This voice carried age. A stillness that had no right to exist here. The woman she would have become.

Thomas squeezed his eyes shut, his body shaking. Was this it? The absolution he'd prayed for? Divine intervention sought in a thousand empty chapels? A miracle here, in this place of darkness? The thought dizzied him. Beautiful. Hopeful.

But something colder stirred. The part of him shaped by years of theological argument, by faith that had cracked under real weight. It didn't trust this.

This was a place that fed on pain. It had just shown him his most traumatic moment with cruel, surgical precision. Offering grace now wasn't generosity. It was a strategy. The most sophisticated temptation he'd ever faced.

To accept this forgiveness meant accepting that this ancient, malevolent thing could grant mercy his own God had withheld. Blasphemy. A trick. Poison in a golden chalice.

He hung between them. The desperate, lifelong need for peace. The certainty that this peace was a lie. He wanted to believe. Needed to believe. But his faith, fractured as it was, demanded he hold on.

The room convulsed. Reality couldn't sustain the contradiction. It reasserted itself in stages. The bedroom dissolved, leaving traces on the stone. A faint ghost of yellow wallpaper. Lavender still in the air. And in his chest, the weight of a choice that couldn't be undone. But it could, perhaps, be finally understood.

Thomas stood again in the cold, grey cave. His collar crisp and white. But something had shifted in him. The apparition hadn't been random. It had been deliberate. It dug into the rawest part of him, exposed the wound, then offered the exact thing he'd been reaching for his whole life.

It didn't matter whether the forgiveness was real or a lie. What it had shown him was real.

His guilt wasn't something he carried. It was something he had built, and kept building, and called home.

"It's not just showing us our traumas." Elena's voice filled with dawning horror as she stared at readings that defied explanation. "It's showing us how they shaped us."

"How they made us compatible," Marcus spoke from the shadows, blood still streaming from his nose. "Each wound creates a specific resonance. The cave is tuning us like instruments."

They pulled Thomas away. The chamber began to shift, stone flowing like water, erasing what had appeared there. But traces remained. In the walls. In their instruments. In Thomas himself.

They stumbled into the next passage. Thomas looked down at his left hand. The tremor had stopped. Thirteen years of shaking, gone. A stillness in its place that felt wrong at first, too quiet, the way a room sounds strange after a noise you've lived with finally stops.

Behind them, new symbols emerged in the stone where Maria's room had been. Ancient words that translated as both "prison" and "key."

The cave had more rooms to explore. More wounds to open. Thomas walked steadier now, and that frightened him more than the shaking ever had.

His rosary beads clicked softly as they went down.

Chapter 14

The passage groaned. A low, guttural sound. Stone under unnatural stress. The corridor split, and a wall of rock erupted from the floor with the speed and finality of a guillotine, sealing Marcus and Father Thomas off from the rest of them. Their startled cries died instantly behind it.

Elena and Alexis stood alone. A sudden, ringing silence.

Elena's atmospheric sensors chirped in an escalating rhythm. "Where are we now? Something's wrong." Her eyes moved around the newly formed chamber. "Do you feel that? The air pressure keeps changing."

The words died in her throat. The stone floor broke apart beneath them, porous and crumbling, and a tunnel formed as they fell. The texture changed under her boots. No longer rock. Something that felt like failing concrete. A sharp chemical tang hit her. Not minerals. Not cave air. Salt and decay. The smell of deep ocean, wildly out of place this far underground.

Then the world dissolved.

The pale glow of cave walls vanished. Sickly, flickering blue replaced it. Emergency lights. Yellow and black construction tape shimmered into view, translucent at first, then sharp. Elena's breath caught.

She was no longer in a cave. She was standing three floors below ground in the Athens parking garage. The final moments before the collapse.

The air was thick with concrete dust. Stressed rebar screamed somewhere above her. A sound that had lived in her nightmares for three years. The massive support columns near her began to buckle.

Alexis saw something different. A rain-lashed cliff face on a forgotten Aegean Island. Gale-force wind tore at him, stinging his face with salt spray. Slick rock under his hands. He struggled to keep his footing. Just a few feet away stood his brother Nicolas, back to the storm, tracing symbols on wet rock with chalk.

Their traumas had found each other.

"Elena!" Alexis called out. His voice came back strange, distant, and echoey, as though carried from somewhere far off, even though he was right there. "The patterns. They're the same ones Nicolas found right before…"

Water seeped upward through the concrete floor of Elena's garage, defying gravity. Not clean water from burst pipes. Dark, briny. Her diving watch cycled frantically. Sarah's watch. The depth gauge flickered between 3 meters and 700 meters. The water rose to her knees with the exact salinity and cold of the Crete cave system.

Through the murky water, a figure swam toward her. The silhouette was unmistakable, even in the strobing blue of the emergency lights.

Sarah.

Her dead colleague moved with urgent, distorted gestures. But she wasn't calling for help. She was pointing upward. Her expression wasn't fear.

"She wasn't calling for rescue." Elena breathed the words. "She was trying to save me. She was warning me."

Alexis watched his brother's final moments from a new angle. He wasn't a distant observer anymore. He was there. He could see the frantic intelligence in Nicolas's eyes. His brother wasn't examining the cliff markings out of curiosity. He had found something dangerous, something that was hunting him, and he was trying to leave a message before it was too late.

"He knew," Alexis said into the wind. "The whole time, he knew."

The water reached Elena's chest. The pressure felt crushing even though she knew it shouldn't. But her fear was giving way to something cold and clear. She looked past the collapsing pillars and the rising water and began to see things she had missed before. Her own calculations. The ones that had saved seventeen lives that day. The eastern stairwell had stayed clear because of her warnings. She could see the faces of the people who had walked out alive.

The cave wasn't only showing her the failure. It was showing her the rest of it, too.

The visions settled. The water stopped rising. The storm around Alexis softened to a quiet breeze. Their shared traumas still hung in the air, but the force had gone out of them.

Elena checked her instruments. Still screaming. "The cave isn't punishing us." Something like awe moved through her voice. "It's showing how our wounds shaped how we see things. Our pain became a tool. I understand structural failure because I've lived through it. And you…"

"Because I've never stopped looking." Alexis touched his brother's compass, which hung against his chest. He finally understood why it had broken. It was never meant to point to

94

Nicolas. It was meant to point to what Nicolas had found.

The shifts accelerated. Elena's instruments flickered wildly. The cave wasn't just moving stone. It was rewriting the world around them, molding it to the shape of their pain.

"Look." Alexis pointed to where their overlapping visions had produced something new, something that existed in the space between their nightmares. The dark, salty water from Elena's memory crashed against the cliff face from Alexis's. Its waves carved symbols into the rock. Symbols that neither of them recognized.

They began to move together, not through a cave but through the landscape they now shared. Elena waded through rising floodwater while Alexis climbed slick, rain-soaked stone. Their worlds blurred into one. Submerged concrete pillars rose like monoliths from storm-tossed water. Emergency lights strobed against jagged cliffs. Nicolas's symbols appeared etched in rust on buckling walls.

Elena watched her instruments stutter and fail. "Better turn this off. Our traumas are linking together. Almost like translators."

Alexis looked at the collapsing garage and saw, for the first time, not just chaos but direction. A path through the fallen debris, his guide's instincts could read. At the same moment, Elena looked at the storm-lashed cliff and saw fault lines. A path of least resistance, her engineering mind could calculate.

"The main support on the west wall is about to go," she said. "There's a load-bearing frame behind it that will hold for thirty seconds. You can use it to climb."

"The current is pulling toward a breach in the foundation." Alexis tracked the flow of the water. "Follow it and it'll take you to a stable section of floor."

95

They were no longer just inside their trauma. They were navigating through it.

Behind them, the shifting mist of their memories seeped into stone, hardening into faint glowing trails. Maps for others like them. The cave had absorbed their pain. They had unraveled its secrets in return.

They emerged into a quiet chamber where the others waited. Elena and Alexis carried something new. They had been broken in specific ways that allowed them to perceive certain impossibilities, and now they understood what that meant.

A deep hum resonated in the rock beneath their feet. The cave hadn't been trying to destroy them.

The darkness ahead was patient. Something was gathering on the other side.

Chapter 15

Victoria Nash's heels echoed on polished marble, the sound cutting through the silence of the university halls. The old security guard hunched over a flickering television in the lobby and gave her a lazy nod as she passed. Always burning the midnight oil, he probably figured. Always building toward something.

He was half right.

She entered her office without turning on the lights. The city glowed through the tall windows, cool and indifferent, and she preferred it to the overhead fluorescents. Marcus had once made a point of claiming this view as his own. She still found that satisfying. She settled into her chair, pulled up his personnel file, and started reading.

His team appeared name by name.

Elena Papadakis. The engineer who had been flagged for disciplinary review after sounding alarms about the Athens earthquake against the wishes of everyone above her. A mind that found the cracks in everything, including herself.

Father Thomas Rivera. A quiet priest with a sealed military record, some kind of past that touched the Vatican, and hands that trembled with what looked like guilt.

Sarah Chen. The marine archaeologist whose last mission

ended with a team member dead. Everyone else came home. She'd been living with that ever since.

And a site guide named Alexis, there to help Marcus learn the terrain.

Victoria leaned back. He called it a research team. She saw a support group for the professionally damned.

"Still surrounding yourself with broken people," she said to the empty room. "Still thinking suffering counts for something."

She moved through his financial records. Her access codes cleared the university's firewalls without resistance. The funding from Niko Stavros was large and clearly rushed. Helena's permit work showed someone trying hard to make something defensible. The equipment manifest told her exactly what they were bringing underground.

She didn't need to go with them. She just needed to be there when they came back up.

Her phone rang.

Her contact at the Hellenic Archaeological Service. A man whose career she had saved two years earlier, quietly, in a way he would not forget.

"Dr. Nash? The Stavros expedition has entered the restricted areas on Kymolos. Authorities are already reporting anomalies. Equipment malfunctions, strange magnetic readings. The chief of police is concerned."

"Concern is appropriate, Director." She kept her voice even. "I'll be there in the morning. Start preparing documentation for the ethics committee. An unofficial, privately funded excavation at a site like this can't go unchallenged."

She hung up and opened her private drive. Air-gapped, accessible to no one but her. Thirty years of notes on the same patterns Marcus had been chasing publicly, loudly, with the kind of certainty that made people nervous. She had watched how that played out for others and made different choices.

Near the top of the folder was a scan of her mentor's handwriting. Dr. Elisabeth Cray, near the end, was writing like someone who had stopped sleeping. *Let this be my warning... some doors must remain closed.*

Elisabeth had tried to hold the door shut herself. That was the mistake.

Victoria booked the morning flight. She would arrive as the concerned colleague, the one asking the hard questions about ethics and process, and by then, Marcus would have already done the work. He would push too far once he found something, because he always did, and she would be standing right there with the documentation already filed.

The patterns in those monastery foundations were real. She had verified that years ago, from a safe distance, letting other people's ambitions do the confirming. Whatever was down there, she would learn what it was through Marcus.

Three years ago, she had ended his career. Now he was about to give her the most significant find of the century, and by the time he understood what had happened, it would already be over.

He was playing his part perfectly. He always had.

Chapter 16

The stone floor lurched under Marcus's boots. The vibrations felt purposeful somehow, like the earth was responding to something neither of them could see.

One moment, he and Father Thomas stood alone in a narrow passage, the walls close enough that Marcus could feel the cold radiating off the rock. His breath fogged in the dim light. The passage stretched ahead into darkness, the same darkness they'd been walking through for the past hour. The same damp smell of limestone and standing water. The same silence, broken only by their footsteps and the occasional drip from the ceiling.

Then everything turned sideways.

A crack of white light split the darkness ahead. It widened with a sound like tearing fabric, and the echo multiplied off the walls until it seemed to come from everywhere at once. Then came a wet, tearing sound.

Marcus had heard enough bones break to know what that sounded like. This was similar, but wrong. Too liquid. His gut told him to run, but his feet didn't follow. He stood there watching the light pulse and fade, watching the shadows twist into shapes that never quite resolved.

Father Thomas had gone still beside him. His breathing had changed, gone shallow and quick. His hand moved to the cross at his chest, fingers closing around it.

"Marcus!" Elena's voice came from somewhere ahead. Distant and distorted, like she was calling through water. "Marcus!"

The passage opened. The stone didn't crack or crumble, it simply vanished. One second it was solid rock. Next, an empty space yawned before them. The edges were smooth, almost polished. No rubble. No dust. Just an absence where stone had been.

Marcus waited for the fear to hit. The vertigo. The panic.

Instead, he felt calm. Too calm. The way time sometimes slows before a car accident, when you find yourself noticing useless things. The pattern of cracks in the windshield, the smell of coffee from the cup holder, the way light catches on broken glass.

He'd spent fifteen years preparing for this. Fifteen years of research of theories that got him laughed out of academic conferences, of late nights in archives that smelled like mold and old paper. Fifteen years of people calling him obsessed, paranoid, delusional. His ex-wife had used those exact words in the divorce papers.

Everything he'd theorized, everything he'd been mocked for, was standing right in front of him.

He almost laughed. It came out as something between a cough and a wheeze. Father Thomas turned to look at him, and Marcus saw genuine concern in the old man's eyes. Not the polite kind someone offers a lunatic. Real worry.

"We need to move," Father Thomas said. His voice was steady, but his hand was still on the cross. "But where?"

Marcus gestured at the opening. "That's where we've been heading all along."

"You don't know what's in there."

"No," Marcus admitted. "But I know what's behind us."

The wet sound came again, closer now. From the darkness at their backs, something was following. He could hear it breathing, slow and deliberate, a faint whistle on the exhale like air moving through a narrow passage. Like wind through a mouth.

Father Thomas's hand moved from the cross to Marcus's arm, fingers digging in through the jacket fabric. "Marcus, listen to me."

"I'm done listening." Marcus pulled free, not roughly, but firmly. "I'm done theorizing and second-guessing and trying to explain this in terms that make sense. It doesn't make sense. It was never supposed to."

He stepped toward the opening. The air there was colder and oddly thin, that hollow feeling in the lungs when you can't quite get enough oxygen. His ears popped. The pressure had changed, though he couldn't say whether higher or lower.

The edges shimmered. Not like heat haze. More like the air itself was uncertain. Marcus reached out and stopped his hand just short of touching it. Something was radiating from the edge. Not heat. Not cold. Something else.

"You're afraid," Father Thomas said behind him.

"Of course I'm afraid." Marcus looked back at him. The priest looked older in the dim light, shadows pooling in the lines of his face. "But I'm more afraid of going back to pretending this isn't real."

Elena's voice came again, fainter. Marcus couldn't tell anymore whether she was ahead of them or behind. The acoustics in this place had stopped making sense somewhere around the third level down.

He took another step. The darkness ahead wasn't empty. Shapes moved in it, or maybe his eyes were filling in patterns where there was only shadow. But no, there was definitely something there. Multiple somethings, shifting and turning, never holding still long enough to focus on.

His hands were shaking. He noticed this at a remove, the way you notice something happening across a room. Breathing too fast. Heart hammering. Sweat on his palms despite the cold. His body was doing its thing while the rest of him stayed oddly quiet.

Behind them, the whistling breath grew louder. Closer. Marcus smelled copper and salt, and the word came to him without invitation: blood.

"Are you coming?" he asked Father Thomas.

The priest didn't answer right away. His lips were moving, but no sound was coming out. He had the cross in his hand again.

When he finally spoke, his voice was hushed. "I suppose I don't have much choice."

"We always have a choice," Marcus said. "We just don't always like the options."

He stepped through.

The transition was immediate. Stone passage, then nothing he recognized. The air tasted different, felt different against his skin. The darkness here was thicker, more present.

He breathed in. Too thin and too heavy at once. His vision adjusted, shapes resolving, still wrong, but distinct from the surrounding dark.

Behind him, Father Thomas stepped through. His sharp intake of breath, and then the whispered Latin, the words tumbling over each other in a desperate rush.

Ahead, Elena's voice came one more time. Not distorted now. Clear and close, though Marcus still couldn't see her.

"I'm here," he called back. His voice sounded strange in this place. "We're both here."

No response. Just their breathing, and the distant drip of water, and something else. A low hum at the very edge of hearing. Like machinery running far away. Like the world itself had found a frequency.

Marcus pulled out the flashlight. The beam cut through the darkness, reflected off surfaces that had no business existing, and cast shadows that moved wrong.

"God help us," Father Thomas whispered.

Marcus didn't answer. He was too busy looking at what the light had found. Fifteen years. He'd given fifteen years to this, and now here it was.

He'd been right.

He really should have been more careful about what he wished for.

Chapter 17

The darkness beyond the door wasn't empty.

Marcus stepped through first. Not because he was brave, but because stopping meant thinking, and thinking meant the fear would catch up with him. Fifteen years of theory. Fifteen years of being called crazy. All of it had led here, to a doorway that shouldn't exist, opening into a space that defied every rule he'd ever learned.

He had to know. Even if knowing destroyed him.

The chamber was big. How big, he couldn't tell. His flashlight beam disappeared into the dark without finding a wall. He swept it left, then right. Nothing. Just more darkness, thick enough that the light seemed to die after a few feet.

He exhaled and watched his breath fog, hang suspended a moment too long before dissipating. The temperature gauge on Elena's equipment had read negative forty before they'd entered the passage. Impossible, this far underground. The Earth's core should have kept them warm.

Should have. That phrase was losing meaning down here.

Elena stepped through behind him, her tablet pressed against her chest like it might protect her. The screen's glow lit her face from below. Her sensors were going haywire. Marcus could see the readings from where he stood. Twenty feet across. Two hundred feet. The numbers kept changing, cycling through measurements that contradicted each other.

"The geometry is all over the place," she said. Flat. Careful. The voice of someone trying hard not to panic.

"None of this makes sense," Marcus said. He moved his flashlight in a slow arc, trying to map the space. The beam caught something. A wall, maybe. Except it was there and then it wasn't, flickering in and out like a bad signal. "We stopped making sense a long time ago."

Elena's tablet chimed. She looked down at it, and Marcus watched her face go pale. "We're not alone in here."

Father Thomas stepped through behind them. The rosary was wrapped around his hand now, beads digging into his palm hard enough to leave marks. His lips moved in silent prayer. Latin, probably. Or Greek. Something older than English, as if older languages might carry more weight in a place like this.

The sound of the beads clicking together echoed wrong. Too loud in some directions, swallowed completely in others. Marcus heard the echo return from his left, then from above, then from somewhere that might have been behind him or might have been inside his own head.

"Which way?" Elena asked.

Marcus didn't answer right away. He was listening. Not for sound, exactly. For the absence of it. For the spaces between echoes where something might be moving.

There. A scrape of something against stone. Or maybe not stone. Something that had been stone before this place got hold of it.

"Forward," he said, because forward was the only direction that mattered now. Back was gone. Back was a door that had already sealed itself, smooth obsidian where there should have been an opening. He'd watched it happen as Father Thomas crossed the threshold.

Alexis came through last. He didn't look back, didn't pause to check if the door was still there. His brother's compass was in his hand, needle spinning, searching for north in a place where directions had stopped meaning anything. His face was blank. Not calm. Blank. Like he'd gone somewhere inside himself and left his body to handle the walking.

"We're committed now," he said. His voice was quiet, but it carried in the strange acoustics of the chamber. "No going back."

Marcus wanted to argue. He tried to form the words. There was always a choice, they could find another way out. But his guide's instincts, the ones that had kept him alive in caves and ruins across three continents, were screaming at him. This wasn't a cave. This wasn't a ruin. The rules didn't apply here.

"Stay close," he said instead. "Keep your lights on. And if you see something moving, don't assume it's one of us."

They moved deeper. Marcus went first, flashlight sweeping back and forth, trying to build a mental map of a space that refused to be mapped. Elena followed, her tablet's screen casting a pale glow. Father Thomas kept his hand on Elena's shoulder, the rosary still wrapped around his other fist. Alexis brought up the rear, compass useless in his hand, but he held it tight anyway.

The floor was soft underfoot. Marcus's boots made no sound against it. None of them did. Their footsteps just disappeared.

A drip of water, except there was no water. A whisper of wind, except the air was still. A distant grinding, like stone moving against stone, except nothing was moving. Marcus heard it all and tried to catalog it, tried to fit the sounds into patterns he could work with.

He couldn't.

The flashlight beam caught something ahead. A structure. No, not a structure. A fragment of one. A piece of wall jutting from the floor at an angle that made his eyes hurt to look at. It was covered in markings. Not writing, exactly. More like the idea of writing, symbols that seemed to shift whenever he wasn't looking directly at them.

"Don't touch it," Elena said, though nobody had moved toward it.

"Wasn't planning to," Marcus said.

They circled around it, giving it a wide berth. As they passed, Marcus felt something change in the air. Pressure built behind his eyes. A metallic taste on his tongue. His flashlight flickered, and for a moment, he saw the chamber as it actually was.

Too many openings, all occupying the same space, layered over each other like transparencies that didn't quite line up. Passages leading nowhere. Staircases climbing down. Corridors curving back into themselves.

Then the flashlight steadied, and it was just darkness again.

"Did you see that?" Elena's voice was shaking now.

"Yes," Marcus said.

"What was it?"

"I don't know." That was the truth.

They kept walking. Time lost meaning. Marcus couldn't tell if they'd been moving for minutes or hours.

Then a structure appeared without warning. One moment, empty darkness. The next, a massive pillar rising from the floor, disappearing into the black above. It pulsed with slow, rhythmic light that Marcus felt in his chest more than saw.

"Is it alive?" Elena whispered.

Marcus moved closer and raised his flashlight. The surface was covered in the same shifting symbols they'd seen on the fragment, but here they moved faster. Rearranging themselves, forming patterns that almost resolved before dissolving again.

He reached out. Stopped his hand inches from the surface. Something radiated from it, heat or cold or something his nerves couldn't parse.

"Marcus, don't." Father Thomas's voice was sharp.

But Marcus had already made contact.

The world inverted.

Up became down. Forward became backward. Inside became outside. He felt himself falling in every direction at once, his mind grinding against spatial relationships that couldn't exist. He saw the chamber from a thousand angles simultaneously. Saw himself standing there, hand flat against the pillar. Saw himself from the outside. Then from somewhere that had no name.

And saw what this place was.

Not a room. Not a space. Something had torn here, a long time ago, and whatever had torn it wanted the hole to stay open. It had been waiting. He didn't know how he knew that. He just did.

Marcus pulled his hand back. The world snapped back, and he staggered, nearly fell. Elena caught his arm.

"What did you see?" she asked.

Marcus opened his mouth. The words wouldn't come. How could he explain seeing himself from angles that didn't exist? How could he describe a space that was infinite and claustrophobic at the same time?

"Everything," he finally said. "I saw everything."

Behind them, Alexis spoke for the first time since entering

the chamber. His voice was different now. Hollow. Like he was somewhere else, and the voice had arrived here without him.

"It knows we're here," he said. "It's been waiting for us."

Marcus turned to look at him and felt his stomach drop. Alexis's eyes had changed. The pupils were too wide, reflecting light they had no business reflecting. And behind them, something moved. Something that wasn't Alexis.

"Run," Marcus said.

Nobody moved.

"Run!" he shouted, and this time, they did.

Chapter 18

The library let them go, but only barely. They moved through the newly formed passages in shared, ringing shock, their footsteps echoing in rhythms that didn't match their movements. The knowledge they had taken from the dark gospel had settled into their bones like a chill that wouldn't leave. It spread through marrow and muscle until every joint ached with things too large for flesh to hold.

The stone walls pulsed with a slow internal light that felt less like illumination and more like observation. Like being studied. Like being dissected while still alive.

The passage ended in a small circular chamber. It felt like a place to decide things. There was no text here, no scroll or artifact, no external threat they could catalog or avoid. The danger was no longer something they could choose not to touch. It was inside Marcus now. Growing. Taking root.

He stood at the center with his hands clenched at his sides, knuckles white. His eyes were squeezed shut and his head tilted back, as if reading something inscribed on the inside of his skull. The knowledge from the gospel had entered him through a single searing moment of contact, and it was surfacing now, unbidden, working its way through him the way deep cold works through wet clothing.

His hands began to shake.

"It's still there," he gasped. His voice scraped against the silence. "The text. I can see it. Writing itself behind my eyes." His chest heaved. "New words appearing. Old ones were changing. It's alive, and it's rewriting me."

Elena's last functioning laser measure beeped in a steady rhythm, a small voice of logic in a cathedral of madness. "There's mass," she said. Barely a breath. Her eyes were locked on readings that couldn't be real but were. "In the air. The dark has weight. It's displacing the atmosphere."

She was trying to stay clinical, hide behind the armor of observation, but her knuckles had gone white on the device. A faint tremor ran through her wrist.

The shadows in the chamber shifted. Not a flicker, not a trick of light. Something deliberate. Shapes began forming at the edges of their vision. Limbs carved from memory. Hands sculpted from night. One reached for Father Thomas, slowly, as if savoring the approach.

He froze.

The fingers were familiar. Delicate. Patient. The fingers that had gripped his hand at family dinners. That had turned pages in books they'd read together.

His sister's.

The rosary clicked faster in his hand, a staccato of rising panic. He began to pray, words flowing automatically from decades of repetition, but they came back wrong. Echoes in a voice older than language, older than Latin, older than human speech. Every sacred syllable warped into something hungry. His prayers were being corrupted in real time, turned from pleas into invitations.

"The binding requires vessels prepared by specific trauma,"

Marcus said suddenly, his voice cracking under a strain not his own. He wasn't reading. He was being read through. A thin line of blood started from his nose. "Through their broken places shall the Ancient Dark remember itself, rising through channels carved in mortal pain."

The black liquid they'd seen before seeped from the floor, pooling in patterns that mirrored the crystalline growths spreading across the walls. The chamber was changing around them, the stone learning something like flesh. Veins of darkness pulsed beneath the surface. The walls breathed. The floor had a heartbeat.

"They're hunting us," Elena said, watching her structural scanner track the shadows' movements. "They're following patterns that match our individual stress responses. The darkness is using our psychology as targeting data." Her engineer's mind tried to model it, to predict. The patterns defeated her. Too precise. Too personal.

Alexis recognized the quality of malevolence in the way the shadows moved. The same presence that had taken his brother, but refined now, more efficient, having learned from Nicolas. "The decay patterns in the stone are accelerating. Whatever happened to Nicolas is happening to us, but faster." His brother's compass burned against his chest through his shirt. A warning. Or a welcome.

Marcus went rigid, his back arching as though struck by something invisible. His voice grew resonant, as if the entity were speaking through him, blood flowing freely now from his nose, dripping onto the floor where it sizzled and smoked. "When vessels marked by sacred darkness draw near, their wounds become bridges across the void. Through paths carved in mortal pain shall fragments remember their source."

The darkness found Elena next, but not physically. It found her understanding. The architectural impossibilities of the chamber began manifesting around her. The ceiling buckled in patterns identical to the Athens earthquake. But with the terrible clarity this place granted, she saw the design in the destruction. Each crack, each fissure, formed a perfect pathway. Her greatest trauma was being shown to her as a blueprint for invasion. The collapse hadn't been random. It had been designed. A doorway carved in concrete and bone.

"The fragments recognize each other," Marcus gasped. Ancient Greeks burned their throats like swallowing embers. "Through mortal vessels shall scattered pieces remember their whole."

Father Thomas's prayers spilled out in an uncontrolled stream, no longer chosen but torn from him. The rosary in his hands pulsed with dark light, the beads snaking into intricate knots that shimmered in the air like windows, like fractures in the skin of reality. Through these gaps, they glimpsed vast moving shadows and impossible realms waiting beyond.

Sarah's tools, now in Alexis's hands, screamed a final warning. Pressure spikes, gravitational shears, ruptures in spatial coherence. The instruments were dying but screaming the truth as they went. "The cave is using us," he said. "Our traumas. It's not just replaying them. It's reshaping itself around them." He looked at the walls, the pulsing veins of darkness, the stone that moved like something breathing. He couldn't finish the thought.

His words cut off as seawater began to rise. Not pouring from a crack. Seeping upward through solid stone, defying gravity, defying physics. Thick and black and cold with the salt of oceans no sunlight had ever touched. Sarah's water.

The water from Crete. It was here now, called up through the monastery's stones.

They turned to run. The way back was gone. The passage behind them had softened and reformed, no longer stone but something organic that had closed like a mouth. Exits had vanished. New corridors stretched ahead, leading deeper. The cave was moving with intent, and it knew exactly where they were.

"Fall back to the center," Marcus called. He heard the futility in it. The chamber no longer obeyed. They weren't navigating. It was guiding.

Elena's scanner produced one final clear reading. Her breath caught.

"We're positioned in a circle," she said.

The stone flowed like molten glass around their feet, reshaping itself into the glyphs and spirals of a vast mosaic. The ancient diagrams weren't seals. They were instructions. A manual written in the language of old damage.

"The original binding must be failing," Elena said, watching the glowing patterns crawl up her hands, across her skin. "The fragments aren't just trying to reunite. They're doing it through us. We're not vessels. We're the scaffolding. Erebus is rebuilding itself with us as the frame."

The darkness pressed in then, no longer subtle, no longer testing. A physical weight that pressed from every direction at once and found the soft places, the broken places, the places that had always been waiting for something to fill them.

But it did not enter. Not yet.

"We can still run," Father Thomas said, and even he heard the lie in it.

Marcus collapsed to his knees, gasping, the connection

115

momentarily severed. "We were always meant to find this place," he panted, blood dripping from his nose onto the glowing glyphs. "Every choice that brought us here was narrowed until only this path remained."

The chamber pulsed like a massive heartbeat, the glyphs burning with a black, hungry light.

"Then we face it together," Elena said. The steadiness in her voice surprised her. "Whatever we're becoming, whatever we're meant to contain. We can't let it take us one by one."

They formed a circle on the mosaic. Backs together. The encroaching dark pressed in on all sides.

The transformation hadn't begun yet. But the invitation had been given. The darkness didn't need to shatter walls or breach ancient defenses. It had shaped them into keys long before they had ever arrived at the lock. And now it was simply waiting for them to turn.

It found Elena in her fault lines, where the collapse still echoed.

It found Father Thomas in the hollow his betrayal had left behind.

It found Sarah in the drowning silence she had never escaped.

It found Alexis in the endless corridors of his searching.

It found Marcus in the space carved out by his hunger for truths no one was meant to know.

The shadows no longer reached. They entered.

And the binding began again.

Chapter 19

The chamber held them in suspended horror. The knowledge of their true purpose was a silence that deafened, a weight that left no room for thought or prayer. No room for denial. Only the terrible clarity of understanding.

The darkness pressed in from all sides, patient as a tide about to turn. It had shown them the blueprint of their doom. Now it would show them the paradise they had to refuse.

Marcus moved first. Not by choice. Something pulled his feet forward, the way a compass needle swings. He stumbled toward a deep alcove where the fabric of space seemed to fold back on itself.

Resting on a pedestal of weeping black stone was a final text. Not a scroll, not a codex. Something between the written word and a living thing. Each letter writhing across the page.

The pages shifted between states of matter. Solid parchment one moment, liquid shadow the next, a shimmering gas that reformed into text. The cover breathed. The spine twisted. The whole thing seemed to be constantly dying and being reborn.

In the polished stone of the pedestal, Marcus saw his reflection fracture. Not himself as he was. Three versions of himself, stacked across time.

The bitter, hunched shoulders of his past. The academic world is turning its back. Colleagues whispering. Then the gaunt, exhausted face of the present, etched with sleeplessness and something dawning that he still half-hoped he was imagining. Eyes bloodshot. Skin pale as paper.

And then the third. A shadow that gradually took shape. A figure of immense, still power, watching from the other side of time with eyes that had already been changed. Black, bottomless. Absorbing everything. Reflecting nothing.

The darkness stirred. As Marcus reached out a trembling hand and began to translate, the words flowed from the text and into his mind, bypassing his eyes, moving through him as if they had always been there, waiting.

"The binding requires perfect symmetry between vessel and prisoner," he recited, his voice scraped raw. "Through willing transformation shall eternal imprisonment be achieved."

Elena's instruments, those that still functioned, shrieked. Their lights flared a final desperate red as the spatial readings spiked off the charts. Numbers scrolled across screens that couldn't contain them, overflowing into error messages, then into symbols she had never seen before.

"It's not random," she said, breath short. Her engineer's mind was still trying to impose order even as order collapsed around her. "The whole cave system. It's a containment diagram. Every corridor we passed, every chamber, the library. One single machine."

She looked at her shaking hands. "We've been walking through the interior of something designed to contain gods."

Father Thomas nodded slowly. His rosary beads slipped through his fingers in patterns that matched the spiraling architecture of the walls. The clicking rhythm synchronized with the chamber's pulse. "And we," he said, "are the final pieces." A beat. "A specific, cultivated pain shapes each of us. We are the ritual."

The darkness moved. Not an attack. It flowed toward each of them like water finding cracks, a personalized whisper that bypassed their ears and went straight to the deepest, most wounded parts of their souls. It knew them better than they knew themselves.

For Marcus, it brought him to his knees.

He was standing on the stage of the Athens Symposium. The room gave him a standing ovation, a wave of validation in warm, golden light. He saw Victoria Nash in the front row, not the mask of condescending pity he knew from memory but genuine, stunned admiration. Her hands clapped with the rest. Eyes wide. He saw the world's most prestigious journals with his name on their covers. His theories are not fringe speculation now, but foundational truth.

He felt the weight of a Nobel prize in his hand. Solid. Real.

The cave had been studying him. It had prepared this with surgical precision.

"Your hunger is our hunger," the darkness said, its voice a chorus of his most respected peers, every voice he had ever wanted to hear say he was right. "Why limit what you might encompass? Accept, and this will be your reality for all time."

For Elena, the vision was one of impossible peace. She stood in the heart of a rebuilt Athens, every building her own design, every structure flawless. She saw the faces of the people she had saved, not just the seventeen from that terrible day, but thousands, millions. Families in buildings that would never collapse. Children in parks beneath bridges that would never fall.

No more collapses. No more dust. No more screams cutting through grinding concrete and steel.

For Father Thomas, the darkness offered not a vision but a presence. A small, sunlit chapel. Dust motes in the light. His sister Maria was in the front pew, not the ghost of a frightened girl, not the memory of a child consumed by flames, but a grown woman with a face full of peace.

"I'm proud of you, Tom," she said. The voice he had heard in his dreams for thirty years. The one who had called for him through smoke and fire. But carrying no fear now. No pain. "You have done enough. You can rest now."

For Alexis, the vision was simpler, and more devastating for it. The windswept cliff where Nicolas had disappeared, but the storm was gone now. The sun setting in oranges and yellows. His brother was walking toward him out of the mist. Not a ghost. Whole and alive.

"I found the way back," Nicolas said, his hand on Alexis's shoulder with familiar weight. "We can go home now."

"It's offering us everything," Elena breathed.

"At a price," Marcus said. His voice was raw. The temptation was a physical force. Hooks in his soul. He could see Victoria's face, forced to acknowledge him publicly. He could feel the weight of his restored name. So close.

But beneath the shimmering surface, he could feel the trap. The knowledge offered came with chains. The peace offered came with a cage. To accept was to become something other than human. A willing, satiated prisoner. Your personal paradise the fuel for a world's damnation.

"The original binding failed because it relied on force," Father Thomas said, watching the glyphs slither across the walls. "This time it demands consent. We have to choose to become the vessels."

The cave groaned. A low, seismic exhale.

"If we refuse?" Alexis asked. He already knew. They all did.

The darkness answered not with a whisper but with a screech.

The visions shattered like glass. In their place, a single collective nightmare of what refusal would mean. Cities devoured by shadows with weight and substance, shadows that crushed stone and steel into dust. Athens collapsed again, the whole city. Thousands dead. Oceans rising, black and brine-heavy, swallowing coastlines in silent, hungry waves that left only silence. The sky cracked overhead, revealing a churning void behind it.

"We were made for this," Marcus said quietly. "Every failure. Every obsession. Every loss. Shaping us for this moment."

He looked at the others. "So, we decide. Do we accept our paradise and let the world burn? Or do we become what we were shaped to be?"

The choice settled over them like a weight they had always been carrying, only now visible. They could run. Survive a little longer, souls filled with a perfect, hollow happiness while the world outside paid the price. Or they could stay. Surrender. Become the prison walls for something ancient and hungry.

These were not heroes. They were survivors being asked to give more than they had left.

"I spent my life chasing hidden truths," Marcus said, turning his back on the vision of his own triumph. "If that obsession carved a space in me that fits perfectly around something that feeds on it, then maybe that's the shape I was always meant to take."

He looked at them. No pleading. No persuasion.

And one by one, they chose. Not with words, but with

gestures. Elena turned away from her perfect, safe city. Father Thomas let his sister's face fade into the dark. Alexis let his brother walk back into the mist.

The darkness pulsed, slow and certain, exhaling after an age of waiting. Their choice, freely given, echoed through the stone. That was what made all the difference. The ritual could now begin.

Not as punishment. As purpose fulfilled.

But acceptance was not the same as surrender.

Even as they stepped into their roles, each one held onto a final ember of self. They would become the vessels, yes. But not empty ones. They would hold the darkness without being swallowed by it. They would remember who they had been. And that memory would be their last, silent act of rebellion.

The cave shuddered with a low hum. Across space, the scattered fragments of Erebus stirred, sensing their new homes at last.

Chapter 20

Their consent hung in the air. The words hadn't been spoken aloud, but the darkness heard them anyway. It had been waiting.

The low hum of the cave deepened. The walls shuddered. The floor vibrated with a frequency that made their teeth ache.

Ancient script ignited across the stone. The symbols curled into the air before settling into grooves that etched themselves into the rock, smelling of scorched stone.

The shadows moved like smoke. Like oil.

Marcus stepped into the heart of the binding circle. Each step was measured. When his boot touched the central glyph, the ground trembled. Their breath clouded in the sudden cold.

Elena watched him approach. Smoke rose from beneath him. "The convergence is starting," she said. "All the fragments, all the ambient energy. It's converging on him."

Marcus raised his hands. His fingers trembled. He began to speak, his voice not quite his own.

"Let what was scattered remember its vessel. Let what was torn find its chains."

From each of the others, their darkness, the trauma that had made them compatible, was torn free.

Father Thomas gasped and arched back as though struck. He

felt something pulled out from deep within him, pain in a place the body had no name for.

His hands clenched around his rosary. The beads moved on their own, spinning and looping through the air. They glowed with a dark light, a trailing shadow behind them.

The guilt he had carried for thirty years left his chest. In the hollow it made, he saw her. Just for a moment. Maria.

Not a frightened child. The woman she would have been. A little gray at her temples, laugh lines around her eyes, and in them a look of forgiveness so complete he couldn't speak. She was already gone.

The fragment of his guilt shot across the chamber and into Marcus.

Marcus convulsed, spine arching, mouth open in silence. The script crawled up his legs and burned itself into his skin.

Elena watched. "His body looks like it's rebuilding itself around the energy load." The darkness came for her before she could finish.

Athens again. The earthquake, the chaos, the falling concrete. But this time she saw clearly: eighteen lives. The stairwell was as she had calculated. The child she'd pulled from the rubble, grown now, alive.

The scar above her brow tingled and faded.

She went to her knees as her own darkness pulled free and streaked toward the center of the circle. What it left behind was a kind of emptiness she didn't have a word for.

Marcus cried out. Beneath his skin, veins of ancient script moved like living things.

Then came Alexis.

The cave gave him one final truth. He saw Nicolas in his last moments, not terrified but thinking, working. He watched his brother realize what the entity was and deliberately leave the notes behind. The compass. The warnings. Not a failure at the end, but a choice. The last thing Nicolas had done was try to protect him.

The compass in Alexis's pocket crumbled to metallic dust in his hand.

Marcus shook as the third fragment entered him. His outline blurred at the edges. The cave pulsed louder, faster, until the sound was the only thing left in the room.

Elena stared at her instruments. Every one of them is dead. "The circle's holding. The architecture is stable. But Marcus…"

"He's becoming what he was always meant to become," Father Thomas said. The tremor in his left hand was gone. Thirteen years, and it was simply gone.

"What about us?" Alexis said. "Why aren't we part of this?"

"Maybe we weren't supposed to be," Father Thomas said.

"It needed all the fragments in one body," Elena said, getting to her feet. "And Marcus is strong enough to hold them."

The final fragment didn't have to be summoned from anywhere outside. It had always been inside him.

His obsession rose from the depths of his own soul. The hunger for truth, for knowledge no one was meant to hold. It was everything he was. And it welcomed what the others had given. It was the axis. The engine. The only thing that could keep this contained.

His skin became something like living parchment, covered in languages that had existed and languages that hadn't yet. His eyes went dark. When he spoke, the sound came from somewhere below words, a frequency that moved through the stone.

"What was scattered is bound anew. Through willing transformation, eternal imprisonment is achieved."

The monastery groaned once, deep and final. Fractures spread across every surface, glowing faintly. The books whispered. Crystal veins completed patterns in the walls that had taken longer than anyone could count to form.

Marcus stood at the center of all of it. A man-shaped thing that absorbed light. Part person, part container. The end of something three thousand years in the making.

Father Thomas went to his knees and prayed. He didn't have words for what he felt, so he prayed without them.

Elena stood and watched, and couldn't make sense of what she was seeing with anything she knew.

Alexis didn't move. He understood, without having to say it, that none of them were done. This was the end of the ritual. It was not the end of the work.

Chapter 21

The echoes of the transformation faded. What replaced them was a silence so complete it felt like pressure against their eardrums.

The air had stopped humming. The energy that had crackled through the chamber was gone. What remained was cold and still, carrying the smell of mildew and old stone. The binding was over.

Elena, Thomas, and Alexis stood frozen. The monastery's power had stopped pressing against them. Whatever had been hunting and testing them was now turned inward, contained inside the vessel they had helped forge. The deliberate, intelligent malevolence was gone. In its place, something else pulsed. Slow, rhythmic, like a heartbeat on a long watch.

Elena broke first. "Marcus?"

The figure turned, though the movement was wrong in a way she couldn't name. It was as if reality shifted around him rather than him moving through it. He smiled, and the expression folded into too many angles at once, a shape that approximated a human emotion without quite becoming one.

"I'm more myself than I've ever been, Elena." His voice carried his familiar cadence, but beneath it something older rumbled. Like stones moving in deep places. "Every obsessive thought. Every sleepless night chasing shadows. Every scrap of desperation to prove I was right. It's all still here. Crystallized."

He stepped forward. The air warped around him, rippling like heat off hot stone. "I haven't lost myself." His tone was calm, almost reverent. "I've become the purest version of what I was always meant to be."

Beneath his translucent skin, darkness pulsed. Slow, rhythmic, pushing outward against flesh and will. But he held. His obsession formed chains that the darkness couldn't slip. Razor-edged, unrelenting, now permanent. The hunger to know, to understand, to possess what no one else could grasp. Those weren't chains forged in ritual. They were forged in identity.

"This is why it chose me," he said, and something like wonder moved through his voice, though it was not a comfortable wonder. "Not despite my flaws. Because of them. My inability to let go, to admit defeat, to stop seeking. Here, those aren't weaknesses. They're exactly what a jailer needs."

The cost of surviving reached them slowly. The way ice forms across glass.

Elena's fingers found the skin above her eye. Smooth. Unmarked. The scar that had been there for three years was gone. So was the phantom ache. So was the low, constant hum of anxiety she'd carried so long she had stopped hearing it. She stood in the absence of it and couldn't decide what she felt. Healed, maybe. Or diminished. She genuinely wasn't sure there was a difference.

Father Thomas turned his hands over and looked at them. They were steady. He reached for the memory of the fire, his sister's voice through smoke, the weight of what he'd done. It was there, but distant. Like something that had happened to someone he'd read about once. The guilt that had driven him into the priesthood, that had shaped thirty years of choices, was gone. And with it, something he didn't have a name for.

Alexis felt it as stillness. The restless energy that had sent him across the world, the grief for his brother that had never fully quieted, had simply stopped. The compass in his pocket was just metal now. The mystery was solved. What remained was a kind of peace that felt closer to loss than relief.

They understood it then. Marcus hadn't only taken the darkness. He had taken the parts of them that the darkness had attached to. Their pain. The fractures through which it might have eventually found a way in. He had made himself the one complete container by drawing their wounds into himself, so nothing remained for the darkness to grip. It was his final act. They didn't know whether to thank him or curse him for it.

The cave shuddered. A long, low groan, like something settling into its final shape. In the distance, the library began to reorganize. Books shifted, shelves moved into configurations that followed some logic other than alphabetical order. The whole space was becoming an extension of who Marcus was now. A repository of dangerous knowledge made safe by being locked inside a mind that would never, could never, let it go.

"What happens now?" Father Thomas asked.

"You leave," Marcus said. The finality in his voice was like stone. "The binding is complete. The darkness is contained. But this place is mine. I am its keeper and its prisoner. Its guardian and its greatest threat."

The passages behind them opened. Stone flowed to form a path upward. Elena felt the pressure at her back before she consciously registered it.

"We can't just leave you here," she said, but her feet were already moving. Her body was obeying something she hadn't decided.

"You can, and you will." He spoke with the authority of something that had become a structural, load-bearing part of the walls. He was in the monastery now. "Go back to the world. Tell them the site collapsed. Unstable. Dangerous. Let the official record show that Dr. Marcus Stavros was lost in a tragic accident, his theories unproven."

"But you were right," Father Thomas said quietly. "About all of it."

"Yes." His satisfaction filled the chamber like heat. "I was right. And I have an eternity to sit with that. What better fate for someone like me than to be permanently correct, in possession of truths no one else can reach?"

Something in him seemed to laugh, or maybe it was the darkness that laughed, at the shape his fate had taken. An ancient hunger imprisoned by a stubbornness too deep to ever release it.

"Go." The cave pressed against them, steady and patient. "Don't try to find me again. I have what I always wanted. The price was that I become something that could never be shared. A fair trade, don't you think?"

They left because there was nothing else to do. The cave, or Marcus, or both, wouldn't allow otherwise. They walked up the passage, their footsteps echoing at the wrong intervals, and the monastery pushed them forward until the stone sealed behind them and the inscriptions on the bronze door began to fade into smooth, silent limestone.

Behind them, something vast closed around its prize. And stayed closed.

Chapter 22

They came out through the hidden door on the eastern wall, and the world hit them. After the silence, after hours in darkness so complete it had weight, the courtyard felt like an assault.

Red and blue lights strobed across the old stone. The air smelled of diesel. Rescue workers moved in that focused, clipped way emergency workers do, their voices carrying over the crackle of radios. The partial collapse had pulled in every resource from the surrounding islands. Sirens. Shouted names. Walkie-talkies going back and forth.

For a moment, the three of them stood in the shadows, blinking, trying to remember how to exist in a world this loud.

Chief Dimitris spotted them from near the main gate. He was wearing the face of a man preparing to deliver bad news, and when he saw them emerge, it broke apart. He crossed the courtyard faster than his age suggested he should be able to.

"By all the saints." His voice came out rough. "After the tremors, the structural failure, we thought you were gone."

He looked at each of them, then called for paramedics without looking away.

A young paramedic draped a thermal blanket over Elena's shoulders. The weight of it felt strange.

"Dr. Papadakis, we need to check you over."

"I'm fine," she said. "Just tired."

It wasn't the right word. She felt emptied, like something had been removed that she hadn't known was there. There was no explaining that to a paramedic, so she let him steer her toward the light.

Nearby, Father Thomas accepted a bottle of water, his other hand resting on the edge of a gurney. The paramedic beside him noticed nothing unusual because nothing seemed out of the ordinary. Thomas noticed. He turned his hand over slowly in the red and blue light. Steady. Completely, unnaturally steady.

The shaking had been part of him for years. A physical fact of his life, like his own voice. Being without it didn't feel like relief. It felt like a lie he was now living inside.

Alexis stood a little apart, looking at the sea. The water churned and crashed below in the dark, and he watched it without urgency, without the frantic searching energy that had driven him across half the world and into this place. He pulled his brother's compass from his pocket. The needle pointed north. It was just a compass now.

"Where are Dr. Stavros and Professor Chen?" Dimitris was doing a headcount, voice sharpening. "Your permits listed five people."

They'd talked through this on the walk up, not in explicit terms but in the way you can arrive at an agreement without quite saying so. Elena stepped forward.

"There was a structural collapse in the lower chambers. Dr. Stavros and Sarah were documenting the space when it happened."

"The ceiling came down," Father Thomas continued, voice even. "We tried to reach them, but the passages sealed almost immediately. The whole lower structure is unstable. You would have picked up the tremors on the seismograph."

Not a lie, exactly. The passages had sealed. Marcus was unreachable. The words just implied something different than the truth.

Abbot Kyrillos had moved to the edge of the crowd. He looked at them the way he had the first time, reading past the surface. He saw the missing wounds, the stillness, the hollow peace of people who had come through something that doesn't have a name. He didn't say anything for a moment.

"The island takes what it will," he said. "And sometimes, it gives in return."

Dimitris wasn't finished. "We'll need full statements. Medical records." His eyes moved over the three of them, the look of a man who suspects something without knowing what. "You all seem changed."

"That's what almost dying does," Elena said. Her own voice surprised her with how steady it sounded.

They gave their statements separately. They hit the same beats, same careful phrasing, same account from three different angles. Equipment failure. Seismic anomalies. A sudden collapse in the final chamber. Two colleagues lost before anyone could react, the passages sealed behind them.

Dimitris didn't believe them, or not entirely. But the seismograph backed up the tremors. Their surface equipment showed the energy spikes. And there was no trace of Marcus Stavros. No body, no belongings, nothing.

"Their bodies?" he pressed.

"Buried under tons of stone," Alexis said. "Along with all our research."

The satellite phone rang at 3:47 AM. Helena was already awake, had been for hours, sitting with contract revisions she couldn't make herself read. Liability clauses. Permit language. The careful legal architecture she'd built to protect Marcus from his own worst instincts.

She knew before she answered. The hour told her. So did something else, a weight that had settled in her chest around midnight and hadn't shifted.

"This is Helena."

"Ms. Stavros, this is Chief Dimitris on Kymolos." A pause. The kind that comes before words that rearrange things. "There's been an incident at the monastery. A structural collapse. I'm afraid..."

"Marcus." Not a question.

"We haven't recovered a body yet. The team that made it out... Dr. Papadakis said he was in the final chamber when..."

She stopped listening. Not from shock. More because she already knew. She'd been knowing for hours.

She thought about Marcus at twenty-three, hands still dirty from his first real excavation, holding up a pottery shard like it was something sacred. "Look at the glaze pattern. This changes everything we thought we knew about trade routes." The certainty in his voice. The joy.

Marcus, on their wedding night, whispered theories about ancient astronomical knowledge while she laughed and pulled him closer. "You're thinking about dead civilizations right now?" "Eternal mysteries," he'd corrected. "There's a difference."

Marcus crossed a lawyer's desk, hollow-eyed, while she signed the papers. "You're choosing ruins over us." "I'm choosing truth. I wish I could explain why that matters so much."

"Ms. Stavros?" Dimitris again. "Are you still there?"

"What exactly did Elena say? About his final moments."

"That he'd found what he was looking for, and then the ceiling came in around them."

Helena closed her eyes. Of course, he wouldn't have left. That was Marcus. One more measurement, one more photograph, one more piece of evidence.

"The others are all right? Elena, Father Thomas, Alexis?"

"Shaken but alive. Dr. Papadakis asked me to tell you it was quick. That he didn't suffer."

She recognized the lie. A kindness wrapped in official language. Elena was protecting her from something. From what?

"I need to speak with them in person."

"Of course. I can arrange…"

"I'm taking the first ferry to Kymolos. Don't let them leave the island before I get there."

"Ms. Stavros, I'm not sure I can actually do that…"

"Chief Dimitris." The voice that had won her a dozen cases she had no business winning. "My ex-husband is buried under a mountain. The least you can do is let me hear it from the people who were with him. I'll be there by noon."

She hung up.

She stood there a moment, breathing. In through the nose. Out through the mouth.

Marcus was gone. The brilliant, infuriating, obsessive man

she'd never really stopped loving. Buried in pursuit of the thing she'd spent years asking him to let go. She already knew he'd have considered it a fair trade, which made it worse somehow, not better.

The photograph on the nightstand showed him on a beach in Crete, gap-toothed and grinning, holding up a starfish. Before the obsession had fully taken hold.

"You stubborn bastard," she said quietly. "You actually did it."

She started packing. Whatever had really happened in that monastery, she was going to look Elena in the eyes and know. Fifteen years with Marcus had taught her at least that much. The truest things were the ones people worked hardest to hide.

The ferry left at seven.

Victoria Nash's helicopter set down the next morning with a precision that felt like a statement. The rotor scattered papers, sending the monks shielding their eyes.

She crossed the courtyard in a perfectly tailored black suit, her expression arranged into something sympathetic. She'd come to collect, Elena could see it. Ready to take Marcus's final failure and use it as the last word in an argument that had run for decades.

She stopped short when she saw them.

The people from their last meeting in Athens were gone. Elena stood straight, eyes direct. Father Thomas held his coffee without trembling. Alexis watched Victoria approach without the restless, searching energy that had always been part of him. They weren't grieving. They were calm in a way that had nothing to do with recovery, and she could see it bothered her.

"I assume you're here about the accident," Elena said.

"Yes." Victoria studied them. "Unfortunate. I suppose Dr. Stavros's research dies with him."

"Completely," Elena said, handing over the preliminary report. "The site is too unstable for further work. The Abbot has already petitioned the government to seal the lower chambers."

Victoria read the documents. Her academic instincts kept flagging something she couldn't quite locate, not on the page but in their faces. These were not the faces of people who had watched their colleague die for nothing.

"His theories," she said. "The pre-Christian architectural patterns."

"Unproven," Father Thomas said. "Whatever Marcus believed he'd found is buried with him. The record will show that he died pursuing theories that couldn't be substantiated."

It was exactly what Victoria had come for. And yet it felt like nothing. Like ash in her mouth. She'd expected broken people insisting Marcus had been right. Instead, she'd found something she couldn't argue with, an acceptance that ran deeper than resignation. Like they knew something she would never know, and had decided, calmly, that they were fine with that.

"The university will need to be notified," she said. "Arrangements will have to be made."

"We'll handle it," Elena said, taking the report back. "Marcus would have wanted the site sealed. No future expeditions."

Victoria left without what she'd come for. They watched her helicopter shrink into the morning sky.

As the sun went down over Kymolos, the three of them stood together in the courtyard one last time. The emergency vehicles were gone. The rescue workers had cleared out. Only the monks remained, moving through their evening routine as if the world had not almost ended beneath their feet.

"He took the whole weight of it," Alexis said. "So, nobody else would have to."

"And he got what he wanted," Elena said. "Proof he was right. Knowledge nobody else will ever possess." A beat. "For Marcus, that might actually be the closest thing to paradise."

Father Thomas led them in a quiet prayer. Not for the dead. For the transformed. For a man who had become something beyond the reach of prayers, but perhaps not beyond gratitude.

The monastery bells rang out as they prepared to leave. Clear and measured, nothing like the warped tolling they'd heard on their way down into the dark.

Chapter 23

One month later, a small group gathered in a quiet chapel overlooking the sea. The white walls stood bright against the Mediterranean blue. The building was old, its plaster cracking where the salt air had worked its patient erosion. Inside, light came through narrow windows and threw amber rectangles across the worn wooden pews.

Niko Stavros stood at the entrance. His usual designer suit was gone, replaced by a plain black one. He looked smaller without the armor of wealth and confidence. Shoulders slumped, hands trembling slightly around the brim of his hat. The hands that had signed a thousand contracts and closed a hundred deals. He'd been standing there ten minutes, unable to take the final step across the threshold.

Inside, Helena waited, her face pale but composed. Plain black dress, no jewelry except her wedding ring, the one she'd kept on through the divorce. She held a photograph faded with age. The three of them, somewhere on vacation. Marcus couldn't have been more than twenty-five, grinning with a starfish held up like a trophy. Niko stood beside him, protective even then.

"You came," Helena said softly as Niko finally entered. His footsteps echoed in the nearly empty space.

"He was my brother." Niko's voice cracked on the last word. "Despite everything. All those years of competing. Trying to prove I was the one who'd made it." He paused. "And now..."

He didn't finish. Helena took his hand, and they stood together in the grief that belongs to people who loved the same difficult person.

Father Thomas conducted a service for a man whose body would never be recovered, whose fate could never be spoken aloud. He stood at the simple altar with his hands resting on the worn wood, each word chosen with care. Double-meaning truth for those who knew, and comfort for those who didn't.

"Marcus Stavros was a seeker," he began. "In an age of easy answers, he asked the difficult questions. He went into the shadows where others didn't. He believed the world held things we'd forgotten. Truths we'd buried, not because they were false, but because they were too heavy to carry."

Elena sat in the front pew with her back straight. She was thinking of Marcus in those final moments.

"He did not speak of death," Father Thomas continued, "but of transformation. Sacrifice that looked like failure from the outside but wasn't. An obsession so complete it became something like duty."

When the eulogy came, Elena walked to the small lectern. She'd written and rewritten it a dozen times, trying to find the line between what could be said and what had to stay hidden. In the end, she landed on a truth so complete it would read as a metaphor.

"Marcus Stavros dedicated his life to uncovering things the world had forgotten," she said. Her voice held steady in the silent chapel. "He believed our most ancient places held knowledge we'd lost the ability to read. He was mocked for it.

Dismissed by people who could not see what he saw."

She paused. Her eyes found Victoria Nash in the back row. The older woman sat rigid, face unreadable.

"And he was right." Elena let it sit in the air for a moment. "He found what he was looking for. And he chose to protect it, at a cost most of us can't imagine. His name, his legacy, all of it."

After the service, while the small crowd dispersed into the bright afternoon, the inner circle gathered on the clifftop. Elena, Alexis, Father Thomas, Niko, Helena, Abbot Kyrillos. The wind off the sea smelled of salt and wild herbs. Below, waves broke against ancient rocks in their usual rhythm.

Kyrillos had made the journey from the monastery despite his age.

"Your brother was not a victim," he told Niko. His gaze was fixed on the hazy silhouette of Kymolos on the horizon. "He was chosen. Not by us. Not by any human agency. He had purpose."

"A purpose," Niko said. "To die in a dark cave staring at old papers."

Helena started to cry then. Quiet and genuine. Not for a man who was lost, but for one who had found himself, finally and terribly. "He got what he wanted," she said through the tears. "Knowledge. Something like vindication. Even if he'll never really know it."

"There's always a cost," Father Thomas said softly.

"One he'd have paid gladly." A fierce note in Helena's voice. "You weren't there. You didn't see how happy he was."

Across the city, Victoria Nash stood alone in her university office. The morning light was harsh. It cast long shadows over thirty years of accumulated work. Every degree, every award felt hollow as she stared at the final expedition report on her desk.

Structural collapse. Equipment failure. Dr. Marcus Stavros, presumed dead.

Clinical. Precise. Exactly what she had engineered. What she had wanted, if she was being honest with herself in the quiet of this terrible morning.

So why wasn't she satisfied?

She pulled up her private files. Thirty years of her own meticulous, secret research into the same patterns Marcus had pursued so publicly, so recklessly. All of it hers now. His name would become a footnote, a cautionary tale. Her name would be on the discovery. Proper methodology. Peer review. Institutional support. Everything Marcus had never had.

Her fingers hovered over the keyboard. One email, and her team could be at the monastery within days. She had the permits, the funding, the backing he never secured.

But she hesitated.

She pulled up the medical reports her contact had leaked from the island clinic. Whatever happened in those caves had not only killed Marcus. It had healed the rest of them, apparently. In ways the doctors couldn't account for.

"He found it," she said to the empty room.

She sat in front of the screen for a long time. The cursor blinked. Then, moving slowly, she dragged thirty years of work to the trash icon. Notes, photographs, analysis. All of it.

"Empty trash?" the computer asked.

Her finger rested above the key. Her life's work. Gone for good if she pressed it.

She pressed it.

She didn't know exactly what she felt. Not triumph. Not

even relief. Something closer to the feeling at the end of a very long argument. Marcus had already paid what she now realized she wasn't willing to pay. That was enough.

From the deck of the last ferry leaving Kymolos, Niko stood at the rail and watched the island disappear into the evening mist. The monastery looked small now, an unassuming ruin on a distant cliff. Just another piece of Greece's endless history. But he knew what was underneath.

The sun was going down, amber and rose across the water. He thought about the years of competing with Marcus. The deals, the developments, the empire built from stone and ambition. None of it was what he'd thought it was. Not compared to this.

"Goodbye, Marcus," he said quietly. "You are magnificent, impossible bastard. You actually did it."

Nothing answered. Only the sea.

But somewhere far below, past the sealed passages and the transformed library, past things that had stopped being rooms in any normal sense, something stirred. A presence. An awareness.

Niko felt it and understood.

Marcus had always needed the last word. He would keep it now.

Niko turned away from the rail. Tomorrow he'd go back to his life, his business, the ordinary accumulations of a person who hadn't done what his brother did. But he'd carry this. Not the mystery of it, not the horror. Just the fact that Marcus had found exactly what he'd been looking for, and that when he got there, he'd been glad.

And in the deep places beneath an island chapel, Dr. Marcus Stavros smiled his terrible, eternal smile, and kept his watch.

Author's Note

Thank you for reading *The Outward Shows the Least*. To those who've followed my work from *When Fortune Knocks*, I'm grateful for your continued support. Knowing readers connect with my stories keeps me motivated to explore new territories in my writing.

I originally set out to write a story about dreams, but as I wrote, it slowly evolved into the archaeological thriller you've just read. Sometimes the story knows where it wants to go better than the author does. I was deep into Stephen King and Jeff VanderMeer at the time, and their influence on atmosphere and the uncanny hopefully seeped into these pages. While I'm not sure if I'll continue in this genre, I found myself drawn to exploring how obsession and academic ambition can lead us down paths we never intended to walk.

I'm currently working on projects closer to literary fiction. One follows a chaotic weekend at a DC hotel, another follows an orphan discovering their birth mother's art in a foreign country, and the last is a collection of short stories. There's also a story about a squirrel that may or may not see the light of day.

Customer reviews allow independent authors to continue sharing their stories. If you enjoyed this book, please leave a review on your chosen platform.

With gratitude, Milan Gotcher

www.ingramcontent.com/pod-product-compliance
Lightning Source LLC
Chambersburg PA
CBHW050406110726
47899CB00008B/2672